THE MOLLY O'HANLON ADVENTURES

BOOK ONE: MYSTERY ON THE HIGH SEAS

Academic Resources Press

THE MOLLY O'HANLON ADVENTURES

BOOK ONE: MYSTERY ON THE HIGH SEAS!

First published in 2022
by
Academic Resources Press

www.academicresourcespress.com

This edition printed in by: Lightning Source.

Designer/Typesetter: A.J. Walfer

Edited by Tex Calahoon

ISBN: 978-0-6454763-0-9

Amazing Illustrations by Maggie McMahon

Cataloguing-in-Publication entry is available
From The National Library of Australia
http://catalogue.nla.gov.au

For Chung, Lina and Lily, who embody the spirit of Molly ... strength, hope and determination.

CHAPTER 1: THE BEGINNING

I was eleven years old when I first laid eyes on D'Arcy Wentworth, although to be sure I had no idea who he was at that time … or the influence he would have on my life.

All I knew at that moment was fear and doubt, though that had nothing to do with D'Arcy.

The date was January 17 in the year 1790. I was standing on the dock of a coastal town named Plymouth, my mother beside me. We both watched with tears in our eyes as my father was being dragged in chains aboard the *Neptune*, the ship that was to be our home for the next five months.

The *Neptune*.

If I'd known the horrors that awaited me during the voyage, I might not have had the courage to board the ship. But I didn't know. And so, my mother and I waited and watched as the last of the convicts were loaded on the ship.

We were to set sail the next day for a place half way around the world. Although "free people" such as my mother and I were set to board the ship tomorrow, the Captain and crew were busy loading the last of the convicts into the lowest level of the ship where they were shackled to their bunks. They would not be unshackled for the entire journey.

These were the men and women who had been convicted of committing crimes and who had been ordered to serve their sentence in a far-off land. They included people from all parts of England as well as those, like my father, who hailed from Ireland.

The *Neptune* had picked-up the first group of convicts at London before making its way to Plymouth to load the remaining human cargo. Although it had only been a short time since the ship had left London, many of the convicts were already sick and dying, mostly due to the harsh cruelty of the Captain and crew.

But my mother and I knew naught of that at the time.

And so we watched, and we waited.

We were to sail for Botany Bay.

We were to sail for New South Wales.

We were to sail into adventure… and death.

As I watched the crew scurrying about the deck like ants, my attention was drawn to the pain-filled faces of those being led up the gangplank and filling the bowels of the ship. In fact, that was the main purpose of the *Neptune's* voyage, to remove these unwanted criminals from England and Ireland

and dump them far, far away in places which would eventually be known as Canada, the West Indies and America.

In the past, most convicts had been transported to America, however after the American Revolution in 1776, a new place had to be found to send the unwanted criminals.

New South Wales was to be that place.

Some of the convicts sentenced to transportation were allowed to bring their families with them. We were one of these families, my father having been convicted of a crime I knew beyond doubt he did not commit. And so my mother, Sarah, and father, Thomas, along with myself, prepared ourselves for the long trip ahead.

Convicts and their families were not the only ones going on the voyage, however. There were also government officials and their families, as well as soldiers who would be responsible for helping maintain law and order in the new colony which had only been settled two years earlier in 1788.

And then there was D'Arcy.

I had been watching some ladies when I first saw him. They were dressed in finery, and I was unsure if they were there to board the ship or simply gawk at the convicts.

Either way, they made me feel small, dirty and poor, despite the fact I was none of these things.

Which made me feel even worse.

Suddenly, the women started tittering and talking in whispers. One of them pointed, and the others looked before tittering again and covering their mouths with their hands.

I groaned and rolled my eyes.

Such ladies.

Such bores.

I followed their gaze and saw they were looking at one of the men milling among the crowd. He was tall, taller than my father even, and he walked with a confidence I had never seen before. I knew many men, mostly through my father's work as a carpenter, but even the ones who seemed sure of themselves had nothing on this man.

He walked through the crowd like they weren't there, or if they were, he didn't care, and yet, at the same time, he acknowledged them all. It mattered not whether they were dressed in finery or dressed in rags, every single one of them received a greeting. It might have been a tip of his hat, or a smile, or both, or for some a warm handshake and a short chat, but no one was left behind.

Not even my mother and myself.

He had initially walked past us however, and despite not even knowing who he was, my heart dropped. He had spoken to all the others, but seemed intent on heading toward the tittering women.

I couldn't believe the nerve of this man. Were we not worthy of his attention? My sunken heart restored itself and my despair was replaced with anger. Who was this man, to ignore my mother and I? Was it because we were Irish (not that he could have known that from a glance)?

Was that why he decided he couldn't consort with us?

I had it in me to call out to this snob, to let him know what I thought of him, but Mother had told me to be on my very best behaviour, that we were in enough trouble as it was, so I bit my tongue.

It was not something I did lightly.

And then he stopped and turned around, and he looked straight at me.

It was like those piercing blue eyes knew exactly what I had been thinking, and as he looked at me, pinning me to the spot, forcing me to return his stare, a tiny crinkle appeared at the side of his eyes and he walked towards us.

Oh no, I screamed to myself, I'm done for. He knows I thought him a snob. He knows I longed to yell at him. He's going to ruin this for us. He's going to have us removed from the ship and my da will have to leave alone, be alone, die alone.

Before I knew it, the man was directly before us. Close up, he was even taller than I had initially thought. His gaze was on my mother as he tipped his hat.

'Ma'am,' he said, his voice holding the hint of humour his eyes had betrayed.

My mother nodded and replied, and I saw the man's eyebrows raise.

'You're Irish?' he asked.

'Yes,' I blurted out, unable to hold my tongue any longer. 'What of it?'

I was rewarded with a clip on the back of my head from my mother, well deserved but frustrating nonetheless.

'Molly,' my mother hissed.

'Sorry, Mam,' I whispered, looking down. A finger found its way to my chin, raising my gaze, and once again I was looking into the blue eyes of D'Arcy Wentworth.

D'Arcy Wentworth introduces himself.

'What of it,' he said, 'is that with others from my country on board this ship with me, the journey shall be infinitely more bearable ... as long as you don't haul me up before Captain Gilbert before I have done anything wrong! Hmmmm?'

I blushed, and my mother sighed in relief, but D'Arcy smiled so gently I knew he was playing with me. He was as Irish as I!

'My name is D'Arcy Wentworth,' he said, looking at my mother but speaking to both of us. 'I have been aboard this fine ship since it departed London. And speaking of *fine*, our esteemed Captain Gilbert is a cruel man who doesn't hesitate to let that cruelty be known. Steer clear of him, as much as possible. Should anything arise, come to me. In fact, anything either of you need while we are at sea, I am at your service. Do not hesitate to ask.'

'Thank you, Mr Wentworth,' my mother said, before giving me another clip over the ear. I gulped.

'Thank you, Sir,' I said.

D'Arcy smiled again and nodded.

'And now,' he said, 'I must complete my tour and speak to these ...'

He paused, then rolled his eyes at me.

'These perpetually giggling young ladies. I shall see you both when we depart on the morrow.'

He smiled at me, doffed his hat to my mother, then walked off to the tittering ladies, the last of the people on the dock.

He would speak to them, but I knew beyond knowing that he would not enjoy it as much as he had enjoyed chatting to me and my mam.

I suddenly had a kernel of hope that things may turn out alright after all.

And then I saw him. There, just ahead of me, was Lucky Gem, the man responsible for my father being dragged aboard the ship in irons.

And the scoundrel was smiling as he walked freely along the deck of the *Neptune*.

CHAPTER 2: THE ARREST

The day my father was arrested - seemingly a lifetime before I met D'Arcy Wentworth - was the worst day of my life. It was a Sunday, and after church we were sitting down to lunch.

We weren't dirty or poor, but neither were we wealthy. That didn't worry my parents though. Every Sunday was a Sunday lunch, dressed in our finest, sitting at the table, eating whatever delicious meal my mother had somehow been able to put together out of the ingredients we had. It was all very refined … until my father started telling stories!

That was when all refinery would disappear. He would leap to his feet yelling, or rest his elbows on the table and whisper, or bang his fist down hard for emphasis. One time he even jumped onto the table, describing a swordfight, no, not describing, acting out! Food was scarce that month, but that didn't worry my father, he was putting on a show for us, and despite my mother's protestations, food flew everywhere! I cheered with every thrust and parry, even as gravy splattered onto my face.

By the end even my mother had joined in, not just cheering as I was, but leaping onto the table with my father, playing the damsel in distress, fainting into the mashed potatoes.

My father defeated the evil villain, swooped my

mother up, wiped mashed potato off her face ... then dropped her back down and started eating it!

This particular Sunday however, there was less of a performance. He was telling a story of a ghost ship that sailed the waters off the coast of Ireland. I couldn't take my eyes off him. I could barely breathe, so into the story was I. I gripped the armrests of my chair so hard I felt like my knuckles would explode.

The story reached a point where my father, the hero, was about to confront the ghosts on board the ship, and he paused.

And held the pause.

Held it.

I felt like my heart was about to burst out of my chest, so quickly did it beat.

I wanted to scream, to release the tension somehow, but I knew that would ruin this delicious feeling of fear and excitement that was ready to explode within my small body.

My father held the pause for what seemed like a lifetime ... until suddenly it was broken by a deep thumping on our front door.

I screamed and slid to the ground. My father did the opposite, leaping to his feet, ready to defend us.

The thumping came again, on the door and in my chest. Staying on my hands and knees, I watched my father nod to my mother then walk to the door. As soon as he opened it we heard yelling, harsh voices, and a sickening thud.

My mother cried out and ran through the house, me close behind. My father was on the ground, blood coming from the back of his head, two police constables standing over him.

One of the constables held his cudgel, ready to strike again. It was clear he had already done so at least once

'What in God's name are you doing?' my mother yelled, dropping to my father's side, holding him, glaring at the two uniformed men. 'Bursting into our home like this, assaulting my husband for no reason.'

'No reason? We mean, ma'am, to take this man away to face the Magistrate. He is accused of breaking into a home, of stealing silverware, and of selling the takings to a most suspicious gentlemen.'

I scoffed. I couldn't help it.

'Not my father,' I said. 'You're brutes.'

That got me a glare … from the constables and my mother.

'Molly, you stay out of this. I'll handle it,' my mother said, tipping her head to indicate I should leave the room. I did, but not by much, and I listened to every word.

'Not my husband,' my mother said. 'You're brutes.'

I giggled to myself in spite of what was happening. My parents really were the most amazing people in my world, in the world. I knew right then that they would do anything for each other and for me. This was not a surprise. Despite the fact I could be a bit cheeky at times, my parents always believed in me, respected me, and listened to me.

'Ma'am, you'd best be stepping away. And it *is* the right man. Thomas O'Hanlon, you're under arrest. Come with us and be judged on the charges against you.'

Silence.

I peeked around the corner. My father was still kneeling on the ground, my mother still holding him.

'Now, O'Hanlon,' threatened the constable holding the cudgel.

My father sighed and began to stand.

'No, Tom,' begged my mother. 'You've done nothing wrong. They can't barge in here and -'

She was stopped by my father's hand on her shoulder, his eyes finding hers. I was no romantic, but my eleven-year old heart nearly broke when he smiled at her sadly.

'It's okay, love,' he said. 'It'll be okay. I'll go down, sort this out, and -'

He turned his head and looked directly at me, knowing I'd been watching.

'And I'll be back in time to finish that story that had you both so terrified.'

He grinned at me and winked, then the constables roughly pulled him away. My mother cried out, my father still unsteady from the blow. I moved to run to him, but he caught my eye again and shook his head.

'It will be okay, Sadie,' he said again to my mother, before holding her close. Sadie was the special name my da used for my mother and he tended to only use it during their most tender moments together.

As he held my mother, he looked at me over her shoulder and smiled again. 'It'll be okay, Molly. And think of it! Aside from the ghost ship, now I'll have another story for next Sunday's lunch. The false arrest of Thomas O'Hanlon.'

'Oi, none of that!' the constable said, pulling my father away from my mother.

As he was led away my father pulled a face at me that made me smile despite what was happening, and right then, in that moment, I felt that everything was going to be okay.

I would soon find out how wrong that feeling was.

***

My father wasn't home by the next Sunday. Or the one after. By then we knew he was in real trouble and would soon be up before the Magistrate to be tried on the charges against him.

The Magistrate was Sir Richard Boyle and, although he was Irish like us, he was a member of the United Church of England and Ireland. His reputation, fairly earned, was someone who had very little patience or sympathy for people who belonged to the Catholic Church.

People like us.

He was a stern man who had no time for nonsense and even less time for people he considered beneath him. And my father was definitely someone he would consider beneath him.

It was not a good sign.

We were allowed to visit my father at his gaol cell the day before his trial. Seeing this proud man with his wrists and legs in shackles made me want to have the strength of a thousand men, to rip the chains off and set him free.

To have him swing me up into the air as he always did, scaring me and thrilling me all at once.

Instead, I sat there, holding my mother's hand, watching my father through the bars of his cell as he shuffled to a small chair set out for him.

He looked so sad, so broken, sitting with his head bowed. The gaolers left us then, standing a few yards away.

And then my father raised his gaze and looked at us, and my entire spirit leapt with joy! His eyes held their usual sparkle and he winked at me before looking at my mother.

'Sadie,' he whispered to her, and in that whisper I heard the strength of his love and the promise of a future together for all of us, a promise I was determined to hold him to. It was such a relief to hear him say the name Sadie, a sign that he believed things would be alright, that we would be as one again, a family.

Then he turned to look at me.

'Molly,' he said. 'Will you *please* stop growing for one instant? I swear to all that's holy you will be taller than all of us by the time you reach 12. Stop it **NOW!'**

I giggled, in spite of the surroundings, and once I started it was like a release of everything I had been holding in, and I couldn't stop.

Which started my father giggling too.

And then my mother, and before long we were all laughing uncontrollably, tears rolling down our faces, holding our stomachs, my father banging his cuffed hands on the bars, making a loud clanging noise.

'Alright, alright, that's enough,' the gaoler said, opening the door to the cell and jerking my father to his feet, bringing back the memory of the same thing that had happened in our home not two weeks earlier.

Seeing the gaoler viciously handle my father broke me. Yet, as my father looked at me, his eyes filled with love, it strengthened me.

'Molly,' he said. 'Your laughter just now is the best present I've ever had. I shall keep the memory of this moment always. Thank you. You, my girl, are going to change the world one day.'

And then we were led away, the sound of his chains clinking and clanking in the background.

I wouldn't see him again until his trial.

***

After listening to the evidence, Sir Richard Boyle placed a black cloth on his head. My mam gasped and whispered that this was a sign he was about to hand-out a harsh sentence.

She wasn't wrong.

'GUILTY!' boomed the Magistrate, glaring at my father, before uttering the words that would strike fear into the hearts of even the most hardened criminals. 'This is a verdict that decrees you shall be taken to the place from whence you came and there you shall be hanged by the neck until you are dead. May God have mercy on your soul.'

The words not only struck fear in my heart, they also caused my mother to nearly faint.

Thankfully, however, these were not the final words uttered by Sir Boyle.

'You are fortunate I am in a good mood today,' he said to my father, 'so I will be merciful.'

This was a good mood? I would have hated to see

him in a bad mood! It was hard to bite my tongue and not say that out loud.

'Your death sentence is commuted to seven years transportation,' continued the Magistrate, sealing my father's fate. 'You shall join the other miscreants who no longer have the right to remain here in our land. You shall have plenty of time on your voyage to think about the crimes you have committed.'

'Where to?' my father asked quietly.

And that was when the Magistrate had delivered the news of my father's and, as it turned out, our family's destination.

'New South Wales!'

New South Wales.

I had never heard of it before, but I didn't care.

All I knew was that my mother said that we would also go, as families of the guilty were sometimes permitted to do. We would all be together.

That was all I cared about.

I knew my father hadn't done the things he had been accused and found guilty of. I didn't know why he had been charged, but also knew there was nothing I could do about that ... ever.

So then, like when I was ill, we needed to take this medicine and do the best we could with it.

Of course, at that time, there was something I *didn't* know. The reason this had all come about. The reason a man named Lucky Gem had turned against my father and testified against him in court.

I would begin to better understand these reasons when I met D'Arcy for the second time on the day before we were to begin our voyage across the sea.

CHAPTER 3: THE DUEL

After the trial, my father was sent to the small coastal town of Plymouth in the southwest of England, where he and other Irish convicts would be loaded on a ship and sent to New South Wales to serve their sentence. My mother and I soon followed and when we arrived, we managed to find lodging at the Fountain Tavern, close to the dock. We were to stay there for the night before joining my father on the ship the next day.

'We must get used to not sleeping at home,' my mother said.

We had eaten a meal, and as the sun began to set, we were readying ourselves to go to our room for the night.

Then there was a sudden uproar. A table was pushed over, and two men stood up, glaring at each other.

I recognised one of them as the captain of the *Neptune*, Captain Gilbert. We had come across him earlier in the day as we were arranging our passage to New South Wales. His hard eyes had chilled me to the bone. Sitting next to Captain Gilbert was the man I remembered from the trial, the man who had given evidence against my father – Lucky Gem!

'Mam!' I gasped.

'I know, Molly,' she said firmly, laying a reassuring hand on my arm. 'I saw him boarding the *Neptune*. There is nothing we can do about it now. It will be okay, I promise.'

I nodded and returned my attention to the other man who had stood and was facing Captain Gilbert.

'You're a disgrace,' the man said loudly, stabbing a finger at the Captain. 'You and your ship. A disgrace, and I don't care who hears me say it.'

'Get over yourself, Macarthur' said Captain Gilbert. 'No one needs to hear your petty whining.'

'Petty?' the man I now knew to be Macarthur said. 'Petty? Is it petty that half the convicts already have stomach infections? Petty that they lie shackled below deck in their own filth because to move, chained as they are, is to risk breaking their own legs? Petty that my wife has to see and smell this every morning?'

'Yes,' Captain Gilbert said, those hard eyes staring right through Macarthur. 'Petty. Extremely so. If you don't like it, feel free to find another ship to sail on. It would make life on my ship more pleasant.'

'It shall not be your ship much longer if I have anything to say about it!' shouted Macarthur.

'That would not be a bad thing,' a soft voice said

from behind us.

My mother and I spun to see D'Arcy sitting at the table behind us. He hadn't been there before, and we hadn't heard him arrive. I would eventually get used to this ability he had to move about in an almost undetectable fashion, but at this moment it made me jump and my heart raced in panic.

'Mr Wentworth,' Mam said. 'Why you almost scared me to death.'

'I apologise,' he said, his eyes twinkling. 'I only wanted to calm you, yet it appears I had the opposite effect. But, as I said, this argument could be a good thing.'

I looked at the two men, who were still arguing, even more fiercely than before.

'How?' I asked, wide-eyed. 'How could this be good?'

'I believe,' D'Arcy said, watching the argument intently now, 'that our good Captain Gilbert will not be able to suffer the accusations, correct as they may be. He shall take it as an insult. There are now three options.'

'What are they?' my mother asked, her eyes as wide as mine now. I loved when she got excited. It reminded me of Sunday lunch stories.

'The first is that Gilbert could remove Macarthur from the ship.'

'That sounds like a good option,' I said.

'It shall never occur,' D'Arcy sighed. 'For two reasons. One is that Macarthur is a highly respected officer of the New South Wales Corp and travels to New South Wales to take on an important military position. The second is Macarthur's pride. He is a strong man and shall not back down from a challenge.'

'Okay, then what's option two?' I asked impatiently.

D'Arcy smiled at my enthusiasm.

'Macarthur shall request Gilbert be removed as captain of the *Neptune*.'

'That also sounds like a good option,' I said.

'It shall also never occur,' D'Arcy said, making me groan. In the background the arguing escalated. 'And it shall never occur because Gilbert is a veteran of the First Fleet, and unless he does something silly like engage in a duel and someone of a higher position was to hear about it, he shall retain his position as captain.'

'What then,' my mother asked, 'is the third option?'

D'Arcy looked again at the two men arguing and a smile began to form.

'I believe,' he said, rising, 'that we are about to find out.'

'I, Sir, challenge you to a duel!' Gilbert roared, the crowd taking up the roar as they ran outside.

'This is wonderful,' D'Arcy said, walking slowly behind the crowd.

'How can you say that?' I asked in horror. 'A duel? I thought you a good man. Someone shall be killed here.'

'Doubtful,' D'Arcy smiled. 'Now come with me, to the front.'

He looked at my mother for her approval. She gave it with a nod, and we snuck through the crowd to the very front, where we saw, at close range, Macarthur and Gilbert standing facing the people.

'Choose your seconds,' a man called.

I had heard of duels before (my father had often included them in his Sunday stories) but they were something I had never seen. My father had never mentioned seconds. I wondered what they were to do.

'The role of a second is to prepare the weapon,' D'Arcy whispered, as if reading my mind. 'It is also, usually, to try and reduce the tension between the two men so as to avoid the duel, but I'm afraid it is too late for that now. I shall get called to be a second for Macarthur. Stay here and remember what I told you. No one shall die here today. Can you guess as to why?'

I shook my head. He smiled.

'Think about it as you watch. I shall await your answer on my return.'

'I choose Donald Trail,' Gilbert said, everything about him reeking of the power he thought he owned. The man who stepped forward didn't seem much better than Captain Gilbert. His eyes weren't hard, but they glinted with evil and he set those eyes on Macarthur, but also on Gilbert. I did not like this man one bit.

'And I choose D'Arcy Wentworth,' Macarthur said, looking right at us. The man named Trail scoffed and said something to Gilbert, who laughed.

D'Arcy nudged my shoulder with his knuckle, then stood. He strode over to Macarthur, stopping on the way to whisper to a boy, who ran off. Upon reaching Macarthur and shaking his hand, D'Arcy proceeded to prepare the gun, glancing at me every now and again as he did so.

Finally, the weapons were ready. I could hardly breathe.

'Back to back,' cried the same man who had called for seconds. Macarthur and Gilbert moved in, turned, and stood back to back.

'You shall march ten paces on my count, then turn and fire,' said the man, and as the two combatants took their ten steps, the crowd counted them out.

'One!'

I looked around for my mother, but the crowd blocked her from my view.

'Two!'

I felt panic rising in me. What if something happened to D'Arcy? He was to look after us on the ship.

'Three.'

I fought back the urge to run to D'Arcy and pull him away from danger.

'Four.'

A seagull cawed, sending shivers through my entire body.

'Five.'

Both men looked so determined, suddenly so proud.

'Six.'

'The Captain's gonna kill that fancy-pants. He's gonna kill him good.'

I looked at the man next to me who had yelled out these words. He watched so eagerly, his face alive in anticipation.

'Seven.'

I looked at Macarthur again. An officer. With a wife. I wondered if they had children.

'Eight.'

Oh dear God, what if they had children and he was to die? How could the children cope?

'Nine.'

I needed to scream. I needed to release the … the … the everything that had built up inside of me.

'Ten.'

The men turned and fired, and now I did scream, closing my eyes. I opened them again as the crowd groaned. The two men stood, still alive, their guns smoking, their bodies unharmed.

A man in a uniform strode towards Captain Gilbert, the boy D'Arcy had spoken to earlier running behind him. I watched, entranced, but was immediately swept off my feet and carried through the crowd to my mother, who was waiting anxiously.

'I heard you scream,' she said as D'Arcy put me down. 'I thought you had been hit. No one knows where the bullets will go in a duel.'

With a gasp I looked at D'Arcy.

'The guns,' I breathed. 'It is difficult to aim the guns. That is why you said there would not be a death today.'

'Very good,' he said, smiling proudly at me, making me feel ten feet tall. 'It is very rare, and very unlucky, for a man to be harmed in a duel, let alone killed. Captain Gilbert, however, is about to be unlucky. By my reckoning, we will have a new captain when we sail tomorrow. Which is when I shall see you both again. I bid you goodnight.'

And with that he walked off, my mother and I watching him until we turned to each other in a burst of chatter, chatter that continued as we made our way to our room in the tavern and didn't end until the light went out and I fell asleep.

CHAPTER 4: THE REUNION

The next day, I awoke with excitement and fear battling each other in my stomach. I would see my father, I hoped, and yet I would see him in chains. We were embarking on a new life, yet it was one filled with the unknown. Near on the only thing that settled me was the image of D'Arcy Wentworth, speaking to us in his calm voice, telling us he would look after us on board.

Then his face was replaced with that of Captain Gilbert, and my heart nearly stopped as fear shot through me. Surely, he could not be captain, not after last night.

Not after the duel.

I rose and dressed early, my mother still asleep, and I ventured outside. The morning was cool, and I pulled my shawl tighter around me.

'You are out early, Molly O'Hanlon,' said a voice that was becoming increasingly familiar. I spun around, smiling.

'Mr Wentworth,' I said. 'What are you doing?'

'Well, ma'am,' D'Arcy said, not looking at me but focusing on his pipe. 'I am cleaning my pipe, so that when I smoke it, the taste shall be fresher, and the smell containing more a scent of wood. As I am doing so, I am thinking of our voyage, and praying for a kinder captain than the one who brought us here.'

'It cannot be Captain Gilbert though!' I said, more firmly than I had planned. 'Surely not. You said it would not be.'

D'Arcy looked at me and smiled.

'No, Captain Gilbert won't be in charge of a vessel for some time. Odd how word spread about the duel to his superiors.'

I looked out over the water, mist hovering, and suddenly I realised.

'The boy!' I cried. 'You told the boy to bring the captain's superior to the duel so that he would be replaced!'

'Hush now, Molly,' D'Arcy said in a quiet voice. 'We mustn't wake those still sleeping … or give away my deed. That piece of information is for the two of us alone. Agreed?'

I nodded. Already this man was starting to make me realise there was so much I didn't know, so much I could learn.

'Where did you learn to be so … smart?' I asked, cursing myself for hesitating over the word smart!

D'Arcy ignored the hesitation, although his mouth did slightly twitch at the corners.

'I have lived many lives before this one,' he said.

'Reincarnation?' I scoffed. 'I don't believe -'

'No no no,' he said, laughing and holding up a hand, silencing me. 'As much as I would like to think there is more to death than we are taught, I don't have any recollections of past lives. I refer to the lives I have lived in this life, if that makes sense.'

It didn't, and I told him so. He nodded, lit and puffed on his pipe, the smell filling the air. He breathed out and looked at me.

'I must go,' he said, 'but I shall see you on the dock. As we sail for the new land, Molly, I shall tell you stories of my past. Not all of it, but enough to show you that I have learned from many people, and many experiences.'

'Have *you* had a duel?' I asked, wide-eyed. 'Was that how you knew about the guns?'

He laughed.

'No, thank goodness, and I pray I never shall. No, that knowledge was gleaned from my time in London, where I trained as a surgeon, walking the wards of St. Bartholomew's under the watchful eye of Mr. Percival Pott, as fine a man and teacher as ever there was, and a finer surgeon. But that is just a hint, young Molly. I have someone to meet with and you must pack and wake your mother. I shall see you on board.'

I watched him go and once again felt excitement and fear mingling within me. If nothing else, I thought, I will have stories of D'Arcy's life to sustain me during the voyage.

A voyage that was about to begin.

***

My mother and I walked to the docks from our room at the tavern where we had spent the night. We carried a small case each, all that remained of our lives back in Ireland. Mam had sold near on everything we owned to pay for our voyage and still have some small amount of money left to help us settle in the new land.

It was strange to know that everything we now owned as a family fit into two small cases. The odd thing was, even with so little to carry, my arms tired. I had lived an easy life compared to so many, and my young arms were weak.

Eventually we arrived and were herded to a spot with other families of convicts. The ship was readied, and military officers and soldiers boarded it.

'We shall ask the new captain,' my mam said, a hand on my shoulder. 'We shall ask if we can see your father.'

I nodded, smiling. I wanted to see my da more than anything, and then I saw someone I had hoped never to see again.

Donald Trail.

The man who had acted as Captain Gilbert's second during the duel, and the man with evil written all over his face. Standing beside Trail was the man that my mother and I had seen in the tavern yesterday as well as at my father's trial. James Doyle, or as he was known to most, Lucky Gem. His name was burned into my very soul. It was a name, I am ashamed to say, which produced an uncontrollable rage within me.

I glanced at my mother, but she was looking the other way. I saw D'Arcy wandering over, his eyes following my gaze.

'You know that man?' he asked as he arrived, handing us each a small mug of water. I took the mug and nodded as I was drinking, causing the water to spill. D'Arcy laughed.

'Oh, Molly,' my mother scolded, brushing the water off my dress. 'You'll be the death of me, you will. Come here now.'

'Sorry, Mam,' I said as she brushed at my clothes. 'I do know him, Mr Wentworth. He spoke at my father's trial, and he spoke many a falsehood.'

D'Arcy simply nodded.

'Lucky Gem is a well-known rogue,' said D'Arcy. 'And he's known for such falsehoods. Right now, he shall be trying to curry favour with the new captain, and knowing his ways, he will succeed. You stay clear of him on the ship, do you hear?'

I nodded again. That I would happily do.

'Trail is the new captain?' I asked. D'Arcy sighed.

'I'm afraid the removal of Captain Gilbert didn't have the effect I desired,' he said. 'He has been replaced with Captain Trail, who I have no doubt will be just as bad, if not worse. Stay away from him too, he is not a nice man, Molly. Both of you, stay away from him.'

'Yes, Mr Wentworth, thank you,' my mother said, smiling her thanks, before asking, 'Do you think we shall be able to see Thomas?'

'I don't think Trail will allow it, and honestly, I don't know that you would want to. The conditions for the convicts on board are not pleasant. You heard some of it from Macarthur in the argument last night, but I fear it is even worse than that.'

'But we must see him, Mr Wentworth,' my mam said, almost pleading. 'I don't know that you understand, but we must.'

D'Arcy looked at her for a long while then nodded.

'I do understand, Mrs O'Hanlon. I too have known a love lost, and the loss is still raw. I shall do what I can. Board not first, but towards the front, and that shall give you the best chance of at least a glimpse of your husband.'

He looked at me.

'And your father.'

We nodded our thanks and left, and it wasn't long before the crowd dwindled and we were boarding the *Neptune*, leaving our lives in Ireland behind and heading to a new shore.

I walked on board, and the stench hit me on my first breath. I gagged and coughed, my mother holding me close, stroking my back.

'You shall get through this, Molly O'Hanlon. If it's the last thing I do, I will get you through this.'

***

True to his word, D'Arcy did all he could for us to see my father. He spoke to Captain Trail, turning his back to us as we walked past the area the convicts were being paraded before being taken to the lower part of the ship. They had been allowed to spend the previous night on deck before being sent below, allowing them one last glimpse of the sky and stars before months of darkness.

I saw my father first, and I grabbed Mam's arm and pointed. She held a finger to her lips and nodded, then looked to D'Arcy. He nodded also, then raised his voice and became very animated in the story he told, engrossing Captain Trail and the other sailors around him.

We dashed to my father and held him tight. I didn't want to let go, but in my haste I kicked his chains, causing them to rattle, and before long I felt a strong hand on my shoulder.

'Alright, alright, let the nice criminal go,' a voice said.

I spun around and glared.

'My father is not a criminal! My father is a good man, the best man!'

'Oooh, we got a fiery one here,' the man laughed. 'Hey George, come see this. This girl here says her daddy's innocent. Ever heard that one before?'

Another man walked over, a big grin on his face.

'Only a million times, 'Enry,' he said. 'Cor blimey, if I 'ad a shillin' for every time I 'eard that, I'd be a rich man, I would. Now come on, darlin', quieten your trap and move away. We 'ave to take these animals below deck.'

I was fuming, blind with rage, and I launched at the man called George, flailing at him with my fists, but he only laughed. There was a rattle of chains and a hand held my shoulder.

'No, Molly,' I heard my father say. 'We must be strong.'

'Not strong enough, criminal,' Henry said, shoving my father and making him fall, not a difficult thing to do given his legs were shackled. As he hit the ground, Henry pulled out a cudgel and hit my father again and again, my screams doing little but making him hit harder. My mam fell to her knees and held me, one arm around me, one hand over my mouth, trying to stop my screams.

'You have to stop, Molly,' she said. 'Each scream makes him continue.'

But I couldn't. I couldn't stop screaming.

'ENOUGH!' a voice demanded, with such force that the blows stopped before Henry realised it wasn't Captain Trail, but D'Arcy Wentworth who had issued the command.

'He stepped out of line, he did,' Henry said. 'And who do you think you are, Mr Fancy Pants, telling me what to do anyway?'

'I am someone who is paying for you to be employed, so perhaps you better think about that before you beat up on someone for saving *you* from a beating,' D'Arcy said, and for the first time ever I saw no gentleness in his eyes, only a cold hardness that made me feel both safe and scared at the same time.

'Alright, you lot, I think that's enough,' Captain Trail said, walking over, a gentle smile on his face. 'George and Henry, would you be so good as to take the convicts to the orlop deck?'

We watched them go, my father obviously in pain from the beating, and receiving another shove as he left. As soon as they were out of sight and the crowd dispersed, Trail turned to D'Arcy, his face losing any sign of calm it had before.

'Should you *ever* undermine my command again, Sir, you won't survive to see the new land, I guarantee you that.'

He strode off, and D'Arcy, obviously still angry, nodded to us and did the same. I burst into tears and sobbed into my mother's dress. I had just received a stark reminder of how hopeless our situation was, and our adventure had barely begun.

CHAPTER 5: THE DEPARTURE

We soon put out to sea and discovered that the first leg of our voyage was to a place called Cape Town which D'Arcy told us was located at the very bottom of a continent named Africa. As with our final destination, I had never heard of this place until our family's change of fortune. But for the next two and a half months, Cape Town was where we were headed.

Mam and I, after our run in with Henry and George, were taken to our quarters, if they could be called that. We were to lodge with the female convicts and other families in a large room tight with bunks. We were told that the male convicts, including my father, were in the belly of the ship, three levels down from the main deck. It was called the orlop deck and, as it was so far below, there were no portholes for fresh air or light, creating a dank, smelly nightmare of a place that many did not wake up from.

I was on the same ship as my da, and yet felt so far away from him.

'It isn't so bad, Mam,' I said as we walked in. Honestly, I'd expected much worse.

'Yeah, it ain't so bad,' said one of the women. 'Compared to the men at least. We ain't chained or sleeping in our own filth like they are. Think yourself lucky, Princess.'

'I'm not a Princess,' I replied.

'Molly,' my mam said quietly. 'Mind your mouth now.'

She put a hand on my back and led me into an area which had bunks on either side of a small walkway. Women lay on most of them but we soon found two empty bunks next to each other for me and Mam.

'Oh no, not a bloody whingin' kid,' one of the convicts said as we walked in, glaring at me. I found it hard not to smile, as she couldn't have been more than 13 or 14 herself, yet here she was calling me a kid! I held my smile though, and stood tall instead.

'I don't whinge,' I said, staring her in the eye. 'And I'm eleven, so I am no kid. Would a kid defy the orders of the crew on this ship? Would a kid lay blows on a man to defend her father?'

The other women who had been listening to our exchange laughed.

'Well now, ain't we got a live one 'ere?' one said. 'What are you 'ere for anyway, luv? You don't look like you'd do anythin' to break the law.'

I rolled my eyes.

'I just said,' I told her, 'that I am prepared to take on a hulking man to defend my father. What makes you think I wouldn't be prepared to break the law?'

The convicts burst into laughter, making me even angrier. My mother, who was used to my little outbursts, sighed and placed our cases under our beds. I glared at the women who were still laughing.

'I haven't broken any laws,' I said, 'as I'm not a common criminal. But that doesn't mean I wouldn't if pressed.'

'Oh, not a common criminal, is it?' the first girl said, making her voice sound as posh as possible. 'Well, la dee da, tea and biscuits all round, ladies, I think we travel with the Queen herself.'

She paraded around like the fanciest woman alive, drawing peals of laughter from the watching crowd, including, I am not ashamed to admit, myself. When she saw me laughing, she grinned.

'You're alright, kid,' she said. 'You've got guts. Just don't think you're better than us, and we'll get on fine.'

I nodded. I wasn't a criminal, and neither was my father, or mother. If we *were* better than them, that was just a fact. It was also a fact I needn't let on, as surviving this journey and being there for my parents was more important than being right.

For now.

'What's your name, luv?' I was asked.

'Molly,' I said. Molly O'Hanlon. And this is me mam, Sarah. Me da's Thomas. He's …'

My voice trailed off and I couldn't finish the sentence. A woman stepped forward.

'It's okay, luv,' she said. 'I'm Margaret. I'm here along with me husband. He's below decks too. You and I, and your mam, we'll get each other through this. Together. Alright?'

I nodded, suddenly feeling overwhelmed by everything.

The girl who had confronted me stepped forward and took me by the arm, leading me to my bunk.

'I think we're going to be firm friends, Molly O'Hanlon, I can feel that in me bones. Me names Ada Tattersall, Tattie to me friends. Do you want to know why I'm on this nightmare of a ship?'

I didn't, but I nodded anyway. My guess was she'd killed someone. She seemed just scary enough to do that.

She sat down on my bunk and patted it. I sat next to her.

'It was a misty night in London,' she said in a mysterious voice. Some women groaned. They'd obviously heard the story before. I didn't care.

Right now, I was transported back home, to the dining table, to my father telling me a story.

I could have sat there for hours.

'The night was cold,' Tattie continued. 'A bitin' cold that was made worse by the wind that whipped through me bones. I didn't care about me though. I've been on the streets since I was 5, so a little London cold don't bother me none. It sure bothered Stig though.'

'Stig?' I asked. 'Who's Stig?'

'Don't interrupt.'

'Sorry.'

'Stig was me one true love. He was covered in hair from his 'ead to his toe.'

'Ew.'

'Don't interrupt.'

'Sorry.'

And his wet little nose would nuzzle me face every mornin'.'

'Why would he do that? And why was his nose wet?'

Don't interrupt.'

'Sorry.'

'You're a mite thick, ain't ya?' Tattie asked, looking at me. 'Did you do your schoolin'?'

'Of course I did, and I always did well,' I answered. 'But none of my lessons were about hairy men with wet noses.'

This sent Tattie rolling off the bed laughing, tears coming from her eyes, her breath coming in gasps.

'You ... think ... hahahahahahahaha ... you ... hahahahahahaha.'

I waited patiently on the bed. My mam looked at me as she folded some of our clothes, readying them for the next day. She raised an eyebrow, her unspoken question as to if I was okay. I nodded, and rolled my eyes, my unspoken answer that Tattie was a little crazy.

Tattie finally sat up on the bed again, next to me, her hand on my shoulder as she caught her breath and the laughter eased.

'Molly O'Hanlon,' she said, wiping her eyes, 'I was right. We're going to be firm friends and for a long time at that.'

She stood and walked over to her bunk, lying on it and shaking her head.

'Hairy man,' she said, over and over. 'Ah, that's a good one.'

I stared at her. She hadn't even finished her story! I was bursting to know what happened, who Stig actually was, and what Tattie had done to be sentenced to transportation.

But my new friend was lost in a world of giggles, and nothing I did could get her to continue her story. Not now, at least. And so I was left to imagine a tale which was surely much wilder than the truth.

CHAPTER 6: THE LETTER

We spent the first weeks of the voyage settling in as best we could. All the other women, despite my initial worries, were actually very nice to us, and to each other.

Tattie and I latched onto each other, that was for sure. She wouldn't give me a moment alone, which, to be honest, I didn't mind. To be alone was to be alone with my thoughts, and I wasn't quite ready for that yet.

I must confess I was surprised at how well Tattie and I got on. After all, she was English and I was Irish! Since a young age I had been taught that the English were a godless lot who treated the Irish poorly! Always had and always would, but Tattie wasn't like that at all!

I didn't see D'Arcy much during those first weeks at sea, as we were seldom allowed to leave our quarters and go out on deck. We were free to be in our area, that was true, but that was about it. I worried for me da, chained and shackled in God knows what. I confessed this to Tattie as we chatted.

'Ah, don't you be thinkin' 'bout that,' she said as she plaited my hair. 'Don't you be thinkin' 'bout that or it'll drive you mad. I could tell you, Molly O'Hanlon, about the conditions your da's in, but it won't make you feel any better, that's for sure.'

I sighed and stared at my hands. I felt so helpless. I wanted to at least see him but I had no idea how to do this … and then I knew! I knew how I could accomplish my goal! I spun my head around, but it was as Tattie was tightening a plait, and my hair was pulled hard, making me squeal

'Molly? Mam called from the other side of the room. 'Molly? Are you okay?'

I rubbed at my head, Tattie giggling away behind me.

'Yes, Mam,' I said. 'I'm fine. Just had a knot in my hair that someone pulled at a little hard.'

'Oi!' Tattie cried, giving me a playful shove. 'Is that right is it, Princess?'

I giggled with her, still rubbing my head. Mam was looking at us, and she shook her head and went back to what she had been doing, muttering something about "girls will be girls."

I smiled. It was nice to have her watching out for me, but Da needed someone watching out for him, too. And that person, I had decided, had to be me.

I reached up, made sure Tattie wasn't doing anything to my hair, then I spun around again.

'Tattie,' I said, and I could feel my eyes gleaming.

'I've got an idea, but it could be dangerous, and it could get us in trouble. Are you in?'

Tattie looked around, then leaned in closely and whispered, 'Princess, I'm on a ship heading to a land thousands of miles from me home and probably to me death. Think I can get into any more trouble than that, do ya?'

I laughed and hugged her. I wish I'd known then that we indeed could and would get into more trouble, but right at that moment I didn't care.

All that mattered was my father knowing we were thinking of him, and there was only one man who could help us do that.

And that man was D'Arcy Wentworth.

***

My first mission was to get myself something on which to write. Tattie was amazed by this. Despite the fact she seemed to know so much about the world and had teased me about my schooling when we first met, still she knew not how to read and write, a fact that embarrassed her deeply.

'It's me greatest shame,' she'd confided in me. 'I know if I could read and write then maybe I could find meself a fine man in the new land. One who would not think me just a dumb girl off the boat.'

'I'll teach you,' I'd said. 'I don't know much, but I do know more than you.'

I hadn't meant to offend her, I had just been stating a fact, but she'd hit me then, on the arm and quite hard.

'Don't you be playin' all high 'n' mighty, Princess,' she'd said. 'I could finish your time on this earth very quickly.'

I only wanted to say that I could help you,' I said, tears springing to my eyes as I rubbed my arm. 'I do know more than you, so I can teach you.'

Tattie had stared at me, then nodded.

'Alright, Molly O'Hanlon, I'll take you at your word. But remember, I got me a power driver here!'

She waved her fist at me and pulled such a ridiculously angry face that although my tears continued, I couldn't help laughing.

She did that to me, Tattie. She could always make me laugh, no matter how bad the situation.

Since leaving Plymouth, I was not the only one to find a friend on board. As the days passed, Mam and Margaret had become close, probably drawn together by the fact that their husbands were both suffering below-deck.

They talked to each other non-stop as they worked. This was good for them, but also for us, as it gave us a chance to put phase one of my plan into action.

I pulled the paper off the wall that had the chores of the day written on it … and yes! The back was blank. Tattie snuck outside our quarters and found a slither of coal on the deck, then we raced to my bed, laid a plank of wood on it, and I started to write.

Dear Da, I wrote, before Tattie interrupted me.

'What does that say? What's that letter? Why did you do that one big? Is your writing neat or messy?'

I laughed.

'I have barely started, Tattie!' I cried. 'You must let me write!'

'No,' she said, looking at me very earnestly, 'you must teach me as we go. I want to learn, Molly. I really do.'

I had never known someone want to learn as much as Tattie did, and it instilled in me a desire to learn also, a desire which D'Arcy Wentworth was to play a big role in satisfying.

But more of that later. I finished my letter, to the satisfaction of myself and Tattie. There were many corrections, but I was happy with it.

Most of all, I knew my father would be happy with it.

I showed it to Mam, who read it and smiled sadly as she handed it back.

'It's lovely, Molly. And a wonderful topic to practice your writing on. Store it away and you can give it to him yourself after we land.'

'Do you want to add to it, Mam?' I asked, quickly changing the topic. If she knew I intended to get it to him right away, she would surely forbid it.

She sighed and turned away, wiping at her face. I very rarely saw Mam cry, and knowing she was hiding it from me made me more determined to see this plan through.

'No, Molly,' she said. 'I'll keep your father in my head, and believe he does the same with me. That letter is beautiful as it's from you and no one else.'

'I 'elped with it,' Tattie said. Mam turned around, and like when Tattie had hit me, I could see her eyes were still tearing up, but she couldn't help smiling.

'Oh, Tattie, I praise the Lord you're here. You're a blessing to both Molly and I.'

She turned away then and I looked at Tattie.

"Time for phase two,' I whispered, my heart starting

to race a little faster.

'Then what are we waitin' for?' Tattie whispered back. 'Let's go!'

And so we went.

***

Our plan was a simple one, but as D'Arcy often reminded me, simple doesn't always mean easy.

And so it proved.

The mission was to get the letter to D'Arcy then convince him to get it to my father. Simple. Two steps to the plan.

Seeing as we weren't supposed to be either running round the ship or interacting with the men, though, it wouldn't be easy.

And so it proved.

I was lucky though. I had a secret weapon.

Tattie had survived on the streets of London for years, and she knew a thing or three about not being seen. She was amazing! Maybe I knew more in the world of reading and writing, but Tattie would have come top of any class when it came to surviving on the streets.

Or the deck in this case!

And she had such confidence in her abilities! The sailors on deck could pass within a foot of her without being aware she was there, and all the while she would be pulling faces at them, or looking at me, or generally acting crazy.

I was *far* from confident! In fact, I was terrified. Not only was I defying rules, I had no idea what I was doing, but with Tattie's guidance I soon became good enough to not be seen.

We rounded a corner and saw two men walking toward us. I didn't have time to see who they were before Tattie pulled me into an alcove. We huddled there as the men walked closer, their voices faint at first, the volume increasing with every step.

'I ain't done it that often,' said one.

'Often enough to have the name Lucky Gem,' said the other.

I gasped, Tattie clapping a hand on my mouth and putting a finger of her other hand to her lips. She shook her head. I nodded, but she didn't remove her hand.

'But this one takes the cake,' Lucky Gem said. 'It weren't only to get me out of me own sentence, or to get me some coins, this one were personal.'

Was personal, I thought.

'How so?' the other man asked.

They were almost on top of us now, and I thanked God Tattie held her hand over my mouth, to not only stop me yelling but to stop me leaping out and accusing him.

Lucky Gem continued.

'This one were about a girl,' he said.

'It always is,' said the other, and they both laughed.

'Yeah, well, soon it'll be goodbye to 'im, and 'ello to me,' Lucky Gem said.

They rounded the corner then, their voices fading so I could still hear them but not make out the words. Tattie finally took her hand away. I glared at her, though I was not angry with her but with myself, and with Lucky Gem. I was more determined than ever now to get word to my father.

I stepped out of the alcove without looking and crashed straight into Henry and George, the men who had tormented me and my father on that first day.

'You!' Henry growled in surprise.

'Run, Princess!' yelled Tattie, leaping out and grabbing my arm. We sprinted as fast as we could, around the corner Lucky Gem had gone, with cries of "Get back 'ere!" ringing out behind us.

Lucky Gem and the man he was with spun around but we had passed them before they could react, and so we ran on, round corners, up stairs, and then came face to face with the man we were looking for. D'Arcy, leaning over the ship's railing, looking out at the waters beyond, was obviously deep in thought.

'Mr Wentworth!' I cried. 'At last!'

He started at the sound of my voice, one of the few times his face betrayed signs of surprise since I had met him. He went to say something then we heard a cry, Henry and George were hot on the trail.

'You shouldn't be here,' D'Arcy said, recovering and pulling two handkerchiefs out of his pocket. 'On the ground. Quick now. Shine my shoes.'

We did as he asked, and when Henry, now accompanied by George and two other crewmen, appeared, Tattie and I were shining away at D'Arcy's shoes like we had been there all day.

'Gentlemen,' D'Arcy said, leaning back against the railing.

We didn't dare look up. We kept shining.

'I know that one!' I heard a voice say, a voice I connected immediately to Lucky Gem.

'Quiet, Gem,' Henry said, before turning his focus to us and D'Arcy. 'Them girls. They ain't meant to be 'ere.'

Those girls, I thought, resisting the urge to smile. I felt D'Arcy shift a little.

'No? Well in that case, I shall check their handiwork, and if my shoes are sufficiently shined, I shall send them on their way, hopefully never needing to call for them again.'

He moved us away from his feet.

'Excellent,' he said, before looking at the other men. 'Tell me, are there any boys on-board who could do such a fine job?'

I still didn't look up, but I could feel the men examining the shoes.

'I 'ave to say, there ain't,' George said. 'In fact, I reckon my shoes could do wiv a little-'

'George!' Henry said firmly. 'Enough of that. You girls get back to your quarters and I don't wanna see you out 'ere again. You got that?'

'Of course,' D'Arcy said before we could answer. 'Go on, girls.'

We stood.

'Oh,' D'Arcy said. 'Before you go, obviously the reason you're here was to work, and so you must be paid.'

He looked at me meaningfully, before reaching into his pocket for some loose coins. I understood immediately, and reached into my own pocket, knowing no one's attention would be on me.

As D'Arcy handed over a coin, I passed him the note to my father, folded over and again, so it was barely visible. Without looking at it, he nodded then looked at Henry. It was clear that both Henry and George had been completely fooled by our little trick but with Lucky Gem I was not so sure. He always seemed to watch things very closely and always with an eye toward causing trouble for others.

Had he seen me pass the note? I was not sure, but I *was* sure that if he had, he would use that information when it best suited his interests.

'Well, then, gentlemen,' D'Arcy said, 'I feel we are done here, no?'

Henry grumbled but there was naught he could do. He left with the others soon after and D'Arcy quickly unfolded the note and scanned it, then looked at me.

'I will do my best, Molly, to see he gets this. If I get an answer, I will bring it to you. I can't promise anything, but I will do my best.

'That is enough for me, Mr Wentworth,' I said. He nodded and left. Tattie grabbed my hand and we ran giggling all the way back to our quarters.

CHAPTER 7: THE REPLY

The days following our adventure seemed to drag on forever as I waited for a message from my da. Tattie tried to entertain me and get me to do things with her, but I couldn't be swayed.

My mother tried to get me to work, and I did that, as to say no to doing work meant a swift clip over the back of my head, but my mind wasn't on the work. In fact, I stabbed myself so many times with the sewing needle that Margaret said water would spurt out of me when I drank!

Aside from that, all I did was stare at the entrance to our quarters. Even the fear of being caught while Tattie and I completed our mission and the snippet of conversation I had heard between Lucky Gem and the other sailor had been forgotten. My only thoughts were on whether D'Arcy was able to get a message for me from my da.

'What is wrong with you, girl?' my mother demanded after three days of this. 'It's like you're in another world.'

And I was. I was in an imaginary world where D'Arcy not only brought a note from my father, but my father himself! A world where he stayed with us and captivated us all with his stories, telling them night after night.

'Oh, Tattie,' I said, and she leapt to my side, thrilled to hear me speak.

'Molly!' she said. 'You're alive! I thought perhaps you had turned into a statue for the birds to do their business on!'

Some of the others laughed. My mother hid her laugh behind a smile and a shake of her head.

'Concentrate on your work, Molly O'Hanlon,' she said. 'But you may talk to Tattie.'

'You would love my father's stories,' I said to Tattie, casting my work aside and facing my friend, both of us with our legs up on my bunk. 'He tells stories that take you to other lands, lands of adventure and excitement.'

'We can get adventure 'ere too,' Tattie said, tapping the side of her nose. I slapped her shoulder and giggled for the first time in days.

'Hush, Tattie! You'll get us both thrown in the brig!'

She didn't answer. She just stared past me, her eyes wide in shock.

'What?' I asked. 'Have you seen a sea monster?'

She didn't answer. She simply shook her head and pointed.

I turned and gasped. There, in the doorway, was D'Arcy Wentworth. He was alone, but he held a piece of paper.

'Delivery for Mrs Sarah and Miss Molly O'Hanlon,' he said in a very formal voice. My mother glanced at me sharply, guessing I had been up to something, but she stood, smoothed out her frock, and walked towards D'Arcy. I did the same, my glance at Tattie one of excitement and hope.

When we reached the entrance, I looked back, and saw that all the women were staring at D'Arcy, especially Catherine, a quiet, shy woman. I thought nothing of that but I did smirk, proud as punch he had asked for us and us alone. He gestured us to follow him a short distance onto the deck.

'I have something,' he said in a hushed voice. 'Mrs O'Hanlon, you know not of what your brave daughter did, and I shall not give you all the details here, that is for you two to discuss. But know this. She took a risk not many others would have taken, and ...'

He looked at me and smiled.

'It has paid off.'

With that he held out the piece of paper. I reached out for it but my hand was slapped away by my mother. She gave me a look that said we most certainly would discuss this later, but then she took the paper from D'Arcy. She looked at him, then unfolded the sheet and immediately clasped a hand to her mouth and her eyes watered.

'Tom,' she said in a whisper. 'My Tom. Oh Molly, read it with me.'

I did. The note was short, but it was definitely my father's handwriting.

Dearest Sadie and Molly.

Oh, how my heart sings with the joy of a thousand, nay, a million angels, and all of them good singers, mind you! Your note revived my faith in all that is good and holy, and restored my strength to 100%. It is not easy in here, but I picture you both often, and send a hug and a kiss to you each night before I sleep.

I love you both more than the expanses of the waters we sail across, and I know I shall see you soon.

Da

PS I read your letter to the men every night. It gives them hope. You give them hope!

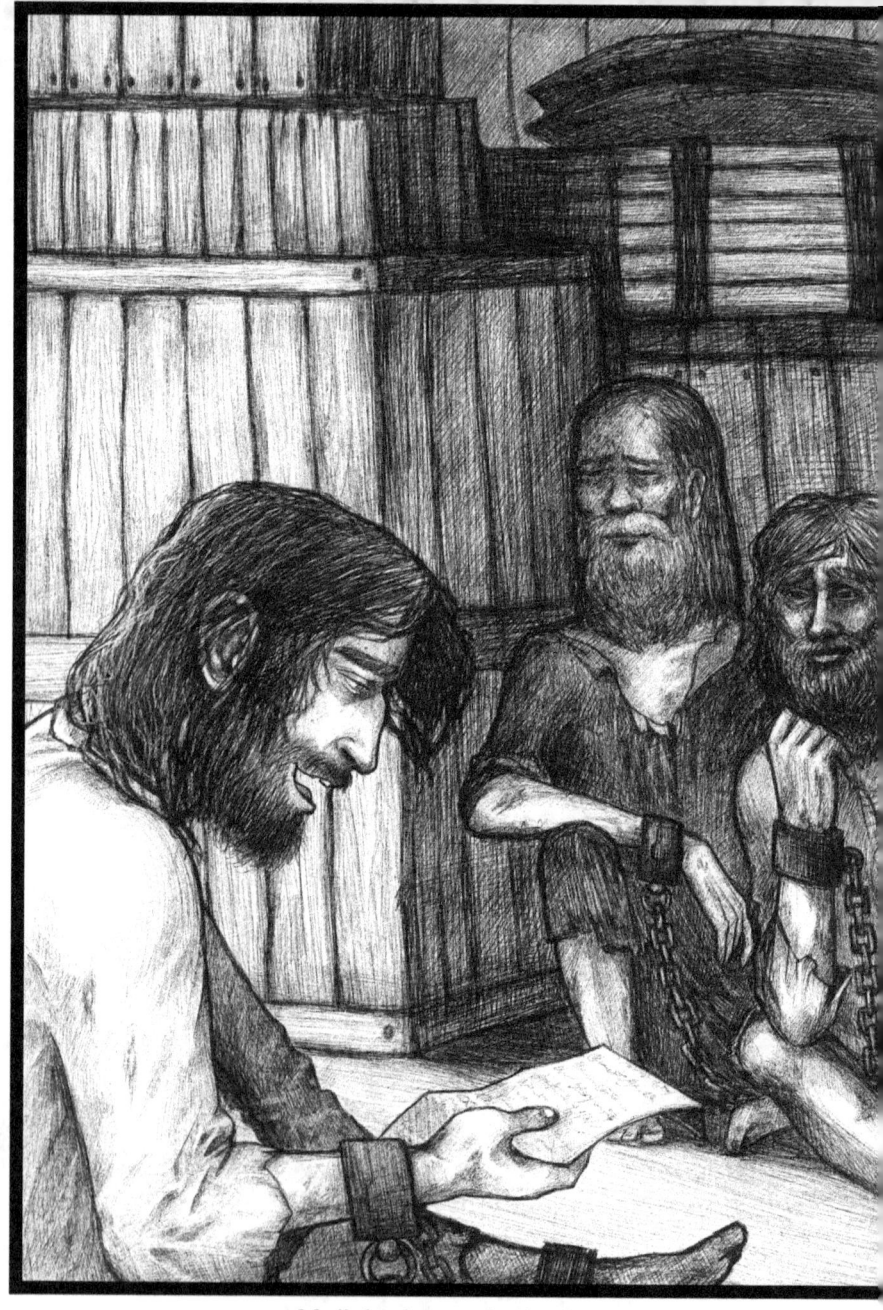

Molly's da reads the letter.

My mother sobbed then, dropping the note. D'Arcy picked it up as she hugged me to her bosom, crying into my hair, telling me I was a silly, silly, amazing girl, and not to ever do that again but that she was so glad I had done it this once.

I buried my face in her frock, crying as hard as my mother, my father's words breaking the strength while building it up. And D'Arcy. Wonderful D'Arcy.

I let go of my mother and spun to him, throwing myself at him.

'Oh,' was all he said in surprise, before holding me tentatively.

'MOLLY O'HANLON!' my mother ordered, in a voice loud enough to be heard back home. 'You remember your place, young lady!'

I heard her, and I knew there would be a punishment, but still I didn't let go.

'Thank you, Mr Wentworth. A million times over, thank you.'

I looked up at him and he nodded, then gently moved me away. I went and stood by my mam again, my eyes fixed on D'Arcy. Something else had made its way into my thoughts, and I could restrain myself no longer.

'Mr Wentworth,' I said, breathlessly. 'You saw my father. Can we do the same?'

D'Arcy looked at me for a moment, as if considering his answer, but then he shook his head.

'I'm afraid not, Molly, and for two reasons. The first is that if you are discovered wandering the ship again, I may not be there to help you. I fear to think what Henry and George, let alone Captain Trail, may do if they find you. The second reason is, and it is hard for me to say this, but your father begged me not to take you to him. Either of you. The conditions he lives under, they are not fit for any human, Molly. You know Trail is an evil man, and this is shown in how he treats the convicts, as animals, or worse. Your father doesn't want you to see him like this, and I agree with him.'

I shook my head and backed away.

'No,' I said. *'NO!* I don't care what it's like down there. I can take anything, anything at all to see my da. And he knows that! Why won't he see me? Why? Tell me! Now!'

'Molly! Enough! Go, before you say another word,' Mam ordered, and when I went to speak again she grabbed me by my ear and led me to my bunk, forcing me onto it. I screamed and buried my face in my arms, feeling Tattie moving to my side, stroking my back, but I couldn't be comforted.

Out of the corner of my eye I saw my mother move back to D'Arcy, and they spoke in low voices. She soon returned to our bunks, and when she saw me watching, I buried my face in my arms again.

I just wanted my father. I wanted him so badly.

CHAPTER 8: THE BETRAYAL

The anger I felt toward my mother and D'Arcy didn't decrease over the next few days, in fact it grew whenever I saw them chatting together. They would stand just outside the door to our quarters and speak in tones that would never reach me, no matter how hard I tried to listen in.

They would speak, they would glance at me, they would shake or nod their heads, and all the while I would be going crazy wondering what was happening.

And so I decided that in retaliation, I wouldn't speak to either of them. If they would leave me out of their discussions, I wouldn't speak to them at all.

But what they didn't know, and what I also didn't know, was that I had a spy on my side.

I hadn't spoken to Tattie for a couple of days either, not because I was angry with her, far from it, she was my only comfort. It was more that once I settled into a sulk, it would take a lightning bolt to open me up again.

And Tattie was that lightning bolt.

As I lay with my thoughts one night, days after we had received my father's letter, I felt a weight on my bunk. I didn't look, assuming it was my mother, but

I did decide to speak.

'I don't want to talk to you,' I said. 'Just as you exclude me from your conversations.'

I was risking a clip over the ear, or worse ... and I got one.

'You'll feel the back of me 'and more than once, young lady,' said a voice that wasn't my mother's. 'Not only that, you'll be sewin', cookin' and cleanin' the slop buckets for the rest of the voyage. And you know how Nancy's innards are playing up so the slop buckets ain't no pretty sight! Now you best turn and look at me before I slap ya silly!'

I tried my hardest not to look, to stay with my face buried, truly I did, but as I have said before, Tattie was a lightning bolt. I spun around so I was laying on my back, staring at her. She was looking at me, her hand raised, eyes bulging, a snarl on her mouth.

And then she growled, just like a dog, and I burst out laughing. I couldn't help it. Tattie was just ... she was wonderful. And now, after days of holding everything in, the release came in a flood and I couldn't stop laughing. I knew the others would be looking, Mam too, and I didn't care one bit.

Eventually, I finished, exhausted, my face wet with tears of laughter. I wiped my eyes and looked at Tattie.

'About time,' she said. 'Now come on, walk with me.'

She reached down, grabbed my arm, and pulled me to my feet. I gasped.

'We can't leave our quarters,' I said as Tattie hooked her arm through mine. 'Where shall we walk to?'

'To other worlds,' she said. 'To wherever we want. To lands and stars and other things you shall teach me about. So you decide, Molly O'Hanlon. Where to first?'

I thought.

'A paradise,' I said eventually. 'A land of blue and green, of sunshine and sea. A land where you pluck fruit from the trees, where you sit and stroke the wildlife, and where you and me and Mam and Da and Mr Wentworth live forever without anyone to bother us.'

'Then that's where we shall walk to,' Tattie said, before striding off, pulling me along with her.

And so we walked … around the women's quarters, over and over again, but in our minds we walked on white sand that met blue oceans. We walked through forests of wonder, with animals never before seen. And we walked to a home filled with love and peace.

And as we walked, as we spoke of these places, Tattie also spoke to me, almost in code, of what she had learned or, more accurately, of what she had overheard.

'They're going to see him,' she said. 'Your mother and the man.'

I stared straight ahead, thinking. My mother. The man ... D'Arcy. They had been working together on a plan to see my da. Working together on a plan ... without me. To see my da ... without me. How could they be so heartless?

This was why they wouldn't let me hear. This was why they spoke in whispers. This was why I was excluded from seeing the most important person to me in the world.

But now I knew. And nothing, not even an *actual* bolt of lightning, would stop me seeing my father in the flesh.

I felt bad not speaking to my mother, yet I couldn't bring myself to either apologise or move on from not being included in her secret meetings with D'Arcy. And this felt like the final betrayal, seeing my father without me.

It was a betrayal I was finding very hard to forgive, and there was only one way to possibly satisfy my anger.

Being held by my father.

It was time for another simple plan.

***

Simple. Not easy.

Just like last time, Tattie would play a starring role in my plan. I asked her to use her skills to listen and learn exactly how my mother meant to see my father. Tattie was in a league of her own when it came to being invisible and listening to the conversations of others and she was quickly able to gather the information I needed.

'You do not need the skills of reading or writing,' I said to her in admiration. 'You have the skills to lead a country without them.'

'But imagine what I could do *with* 'em,' she said, rubbing her hands together and smiling wickedly. 'I could rule the world!'

I giggled and then we both rushed to our bunks, for it would only be a short time before my mother was to sneak out of our quarters and meet Mr Wentworth who would lead her to my da.

The simple plan was for Tattie and me to follow them, letting them lead me right to my father's side. The excitement of the moment caused me to forget

D'Arcy's earlier words … simple does not mean easy. As it turned out, they were words I should have kept in mind.

I pretended to fall asleep early and betrayed myself by actually doing so! Thankfully, Tattie was much more diligent and shook me gently. It took a little time for me to break the fog of sleep and realise what was happening, but when I did I sprang into action.

We silently moved out of the women's quarters, Tattie's training coming into full effect.

'You're not doin' too badly for a Princess,' she whispered. I knew I wasn't as silent as her, but I was certainly improving, as she was with her reading. I nodded, my focus on both staying silent and following her footsteps.

Being night-time, there were very few sailors on deck. We could hear them singing from other areas of the *Neptune*, though.

'They'll be drinking too,' Tattie said. 'Grog. It will dull their senses. We won't be caught tonight.'

I nodded again. It was taking everything in me to show restraint, to stay with Tattie and not race ahead, but I knew I must stick to the plan. If I did not, it may ruin my chance to see my da, and that was a chance I was *not* willing to take.

I was watching the deck in front of my feet as I walked when I was suddenly stopped by Tattie's hand across my chest. I looked at her sharply, but she just shook her head and gently pulled me down, then pointed above her head.

I glanced up and saw we were directly below a small porthole.

'Close your eyes,' Tattie whispered, 'an' look with your ears.'

I had no idea what she was speaking about but did as she bade. I had come to trust this English girl with my life. As I closed my eyes and listened, I heard low voices filtering through the porthole.

And I immediately recognised one of the voices as belonging to Lucky Gem.

'Why'd you call me in 'ere, Captain?' he asked. 'You don't usual call me in 'ere.'

'Because, muttonhead, I don't want anyone to hear us.'

The other voice clearly belonged to Captain Trail.

''Asn't bothered you none before, Captain,' Gem said. 'But tell me what you want to know.'

'It is not so much what I want to know,' Captain Trail

said, 'as what I want you to do for me.'

'I've been and done a lot already, Captain,' Lucky Gem said, a whine in his voice.

'And you'll do more, lest I send you straight to the bottom of the ocean,' Trail said, barely bothering to conceal the disdain in his voice anymore. 'The minor duties you have carried out on board are nothing compared to what I need.'

'What is it then, Captain?'

'We dock at Cape Town in five weeks' time,' Captain Trail said. 'Some will be allowed to go ashore. I shall be one of them, and that wretched D'Arcy Wentworth shall be another. You, Lucky Gem, shall come with me on the pretense of recording the purchase of rations.'

'Right you are and thanks to you, Captain.'

'Don't thank me yet,' he said. 'I have a task for you. I don't like Wentworth, yet I have nothing to hold against him. He curries favour not only with the officials on board, but also the crew. We must set him up to fall, and when I say we, I mean you. If you implicate me, I shall deny all knowledge.'

'Of course, Captain.'

I stared at Tattie, eyes wide. And still they spoke.

'Good,' Trail said. 'I know you have a history of false accusations, Lucky Gem, and this is a skill that shall be called on again. But for one such as Wentworth, we shall also need evidence.'

'Aye Captain. I do indeed have a talent for telling tales in Court to suit my own purposes and have done so on many occasions, sending more than one innocent man to prison. Why, there is even one such man on the ship now who has seen what happens when you cross Lucky Gem. Yes Captain, I am happy to see that Wentworth falls as hard and far as O'Hanlon.'

A knock on the door ended their conversation, and Tattie dragged me off, so I heard no more. But I had to warn D'Arcy. Lucky Gem was about to frame him, just as I now knew he had framed my father!

***

My mind was racing as fast as my feet, but nowhere near as silently. I had to see my father. I had to warn D'Arcy. I had to speak to my mother - I hadn't realised how much I missed her comfort until the realisation that both my father and D'Arcy could be gone from my life.

I had to … and then, when we reached the bottom-most pit of the ship, the orlop deck, every single thought of what I had to do was struck clean from my mind.

I froze.

I stood, and I stared, and then, without restraint, I screamed, and my scream echoed back to me, mocking me as it drifted over the endless ocean.

An ocean I wished to drown in.

For I had seen my father, my mother by his side, D'Arcy standing guard at the entrance to the convict area.

And it was a sight that ripped my heart from my body and threw it overboard.

CHAPTER 9: THE SENTENCING

Footsteps sounded on the deck in answer to my screams, but none of the footsteps were my own. I was frozen, no matter how hard Tattie pulled at me, yelled at me. No matter how much D'Arcy urged me to leave.

None of it mattered.

All that mattered was my father, lying on the floor, surrounded by other men, surrounded by their own filth. The stench was overwhelming, the sight even more so. There were hundreds of men in there, crammed together and chained down on bunks barely larger than they were themselves.

As my eyes became more accustomed to the lack of light, I saw that my father was far from the same man I had seen on the first day of our voyage. He had lost weight, his body and face were covered in sores, his eyes black and hollow.

He stared at me with those soulless eyes, and I thought I saw a flicker … but then the eyes closed, and I screamed again, thinking him dead in front of me, and that was when D'Arcy sprang into action.

'Mrs O'Hanlon, you must leave,' he said to my mother, his voice firm, his grip firmer as he turned and grabbed my shoulders. 'And you,' he said, staring straight into my eyes, 'you must run as though your life depended upon it, which it does, Molly O'Hanlon, and yours is not a life I wish to see ended. Go. Now!'

'What is happening on my ship?' roared a voice as the footsteps grew louder, closer. It was Captain Trail. D'Arcy, for the first time since I had known him, registered worry in his eyes.

'Molly, now. If you do not leave, I cannot save your mother.'

That was all it took. The thought of losing my mother was too much. I ran. I ran and I didn't look back. Not for Tattie, who I knew would be by my side, as always. Not for D'Arcy, or my mother, and not even for my father, who for all I knew I had seen for the last time.

'Wentworth!' Captain Trail boomed behind me. 'I might have known. What was that scream? What have you done? And who, pray tell, is that?'

My heart stopped and my mind screamed at me to do the same, to stop, to turn, to go back, but I ran on. D'Arcy had said that my running would save Mam, and so I ran, and I didn't stop until I was back on my bunk, Tattie holding me as sobs threatened to tear my body apart.

***

I waited for my mother's return and eventually, exhausted, fell asleep. When I woke the next morning, my mother's bunk was still empty. I couldn't bear to think why.

'Tattie,' I whispered to my sleeping friend. She didn't stir. 'Tattie!' I hissed a little louder.

'Wake up, Tattie,' said one of the others. 'The Princess needs you.'

I didn't care for the name, but I cared even less for the intent behind her words. All that mattered was that Tattie woke. I had to ask her. I had to find out what was happening.

She rolled over and looked at me, her eyes red, and I knew that she, too, had been crying.

'I knew it were gonna be bad, but I ain't never seen nothin' like it,' she said, her voice hoarse. 'Never. What they're doin' to them poor men, Molly. What they're doin' to 'em. I seen street dogs treated better.'

I moved from my bunk to hers and held her close to me, as much for my comfort as for hers.

'Why?' I asked. 'Why would they do that?'

Tattie sniffed and wiped her nose on her sleeve, then pulled away a little and looked at me.

'I was told,' she said, 'by one who knows, that the orlop deck, where the men are, is the only deck with space for storage. You saw all them boxes?'

I nodded. They had been behind the men, taking up at least a third of the space.

'That was food and supplies,' Tattie said. 'That was food and supplies that they could be feedin' the men and us with. Instead, they're takin' it to the new land and they're gonna sell it. Captain Trail, he's makin' money outta the deaths of them men, and the more that die, the more space there is, and the more supplies he shoves in there.'

I couldn't believe it. My father and those other men, criminals or not, were being shoved into tiny spaces so Captain Trail could make money? I had a mind to confront him about it then and there, and even rose from Tattie's bunk, but she held my skirt.

'No, Molly,' she said, shaking her head. 'You can't. If you say anything, I won't see you again.'

I didn't know who would disappear, me or her, and I didn't want to know. I sat again, sighing from my inner being, sadness leaking from every pore of my body.

And then I saw him. D'Arcy, standing in the entrance to our quarters, looking at me. His hair was tousled, his clothes awry, his face bruised and his eyes sad.

He gestured to me and I stood. Again, Tattie held me back, but I pointed, and when she saw D'Arcy she let me go.

'I'm sorry, Princess,' she said. I'm so sorry.'

I didn't know why she was so sorry but I was about to find out.

***

'You haven't slept,' I said to D'Arcy as we stood outside the door to the women's quarters. The slight breeze from the ocean cooled me, but the sun was fierce, beating down on the ship as we slowly moved into the unknown. He smiled sadly and shook his head.

'What happened to your face?' I asked. He looked at me, as if deciding how much to say, then he sighed and said everything.

'I can talk my way out of many things, Molly,' he said. 'And if not for that fact, I may not be here today. Unfortunately, you can't reason with a madman, and I fear Captain Trail is such a man.'

'He beat you?' I asked, not trying to hide the shock on my face.

D'Arcy shook his head.

'No, he's too smart for that,' he said. 'He knows of my connections, and he knows that there are those on the ship, with influence, who like me more than they do him. However, he did turn a blind eye when three of his crew had free hits at me.'

'You didn't fight back?'

He shook his head again.

'No, Molly, and for three reasons. Firstly, if I had, the beating would have been worse. Secondly, if I had, it may have led to an even more severe punishment. And thirdly, it took the attention away from your mother.'

My mother.

'Where is she?' I asked, not wanting to know the answer in so many ways.

'She's currently in the hold,' D'Arcy said. 'I did my best, Molly, telling the Captain your mother was there to administer medical treatment on my instruction, that the men were sick, and she was to help them. I said I was unable to go in there, due to the risk of catching the illnesses that runs rampant in that disgustingly small space.'

'You know there are supplies in there,' I spat out. 'Supplies that take up space.'

He smiled at me then, and I swear he almost laughed.

'You are quite the detective, Molly O'Hanlon,' he said, making me blush. Despite all that had happened, despite the fact I didn't even know what a detective was, I felt so much pride in that instant I almost forgot everything else.

Almost.

'Tell me,' I said. 'I can survive the news, Mr Wentworth. Tell me of the fate of my parents.'

He looked at me for a long time, measuring me up somewhat.

'Molly, what I am about to tell you should never be heard by one of your age. I know your friend Tattie has been through a lot, and is hardened by the streets, but I would even hesitate to give her this news. I know you long to hear it however, and I assure you I will do what I can to change at least one aspect of it. I also assure you I am here for you, Molly, always, and will try and protect you from the evils that surround us. This is a promise I have made to both your parents.'

'Tell me!' I said, more firmly than I had meant, but everything he said led me to believe only bad news would follow. My belief was soon confirmed.

'Your father is ill, Molly. Very ill. As with the men around him, many of whom have already passed, he is filled with infection. I fear ...'

His voice trailed off. I knew what he was going to say, and did not want to hear the words, yet I didn't want to tell them to myself either.

'Tell me please,' I whispered, my fingers playing with a stray thread on my skirt.

'He is not long for this world, Molly. I'm so sorry, but there is nothing I or the ship's doctor can do now.'

'I want to see him,' I said. 'Before he dies. I want to see him.'

I looked at D'Arcy with such determination he nodded, then moved on.

'I will do my best, but you cannot get close to him. Your mother, just from seeing him last night, and from being in that space, may have already picked up the illness herself. She is to be checked by the doctor in the morning. So if you are to see him, it must be at a distance. Agreed?'

I nodded.

'As for your mother, she was found mixing with the male convicts, which is not allowed despite what I said regarding treatment.'

'She is to be punished,' I breathed.

He nodded again.

'Tomorrow, Molly. Tomorrow you must stay on your bunk and no matter what you hear, you must not move. Do you promise me?'

I said nothing. I couldn't promise.

'Molly,' D'Arcy said, his voice short, firm, his eyes hard. 'Molly, you promise me now.'

I promised, fear coursing through every single piece of me.

'Tomorrow, Molly, your poor, brave mother shall receive fifteen lashes.'

It was too much. His words cut me as surely as if I had been whipped myself.

I fainted on the spot.

CHAPTER 10: THE GOODBYE

The next morning was the slowest and longest of my life. I kept my promise and didn't move from my bunk, though every muscle in my body strained to move, thinking of what I could be doing to help my parents. Even as I had the thought, shame took its place as I remembered what they were going through.

I had told Tattie, of course, of the fate of my parents. She wasn't surprised, but she was angered.

'I'd like to give that Captain Trail a lashin' meself,' she said, her fists balled up and her face so determined that it took every bit of me to hold back my laughter.

To laugh on this day felt like treachery to my parents, and to D'Arcy Wentworth.

'When will it happen, Tattie?' I asked my friend.

'It's usual around midday,' she said. 'I can't think it would be any different for your mam.'

'Everyone will be watching?' I asked.

'It's cruel, Molly O'Hanlon,' she said, nodding. 'These people, they see it as some sort of show. Now I ain't never seen a show meself, but I sure as heck know this ain't entertainment. This is cruelty, cruelty as I never -'

'I need to do something,' I said to her, inspiration suddenly striking me. 'And I need your help to do it.'

Tattie sat up to attention, not even bothering to admonish me for interrupting her.

'Princess, I would do anythin' for you, today more so than any other. This ain't fair, what's 'appenin', it ain't fair at all.'

'Good,' I said. 'And much as it pains me to break a promise to D'Arcy Wentworth, after all he has done for me, it must be done. Here's my plan.'

Tattie leaned in and I whispered it to her, her nods growing more vigorous with every word I said. When I was done, she stared at me.

'You grow braver every day, Molly O'Hanlon. Your parents would be right proud of you.'

I bit back tears and nodded, then hugged her close.

'Ready?' she asked as she pulled away.

'Ready as I'll ever be,' I answered, my heart pounding, throat dry, hands shaking. But this had to be done, and this was the only time I could do it.

***

Tattie moved through our quarters in an instant,

talking to a few of the other women along the way, telling them quickly and quietly of our plan. Not one of them disagreed, making my heart go out to them.

Catherine came up and held me close.

'If I ever have a daughter,' she said, 'and she is half the person you are, Molly, I will be right proud.'

She kissed my forehead and looked at me.

'Go,' she said. 'May the lord put wings at your feet.'

I hugged her again, needing the reassurance, and needing to be held.

If things went wrong, I would surely never feel safe in someone's arms again.

Tattie raced up to me.

'It's time, Molly,' she said. 'They're all ready, and so am I. You wait, now. You wait till you get the signal.'

I nodded, and in an instant Tattie was gone, out the door and onto the deck, risking everything for me. I cried then, realising what a sacrifice she was making, and without a second thought.

I wiped my eyes and swore I would do the same for her someday. Whenever she needed me, I would be there.

I slipped to my arranged spot, as the sun beat down on the deck. All of a sudden, a wailing started up the likes of which I had never heard in my life. Even knowing it was coming, I spun around to look, worried the cries were for real.

One of the women named Adeline, who was with child, was laying on her bunk, screaming.

'The pain! Oh, the pain! It's too much, it is! It's too much! I need a doctor! *AAAAGGGGHHHH!'*

And then, though I still pinch myself to swear it actually happened, she looked me right in the eyes and she winked! At this of all times! Then she launched right back into the screaming.

'OHHHHHHHHHHHHH! AAAAGGGGHHHH!'

'Someone go, quickly!' Margaret cried, loud enough so the whole ship could hear. And with that, Catherine ran out the door screaming, *'WE NEED THE SHIP'S DOCTOR!'*

I ached to run. I ached to go out on deck, to the crowd, to see my mother, to let her know she carried my strength along with her own. But to do so would ruin everything we had planned, and I trusted Tattie. It wasn't long before I heard Tattie's voice carry back to us.

'DOCTOR! WE NEED A DOCTOR! SHE'S DYING!'

I held my breath, then remembered Tattie's advice for staying hidden, for staying calm.

'You have to take deep but quiet breaths,' she'd said. 'As if you ain't breathin' at all, but you're breathin' deeper than you ever done before.'

It took a long time for me to master that, but with practice I was able to do it, to breath silent breaths that kept my heart rate, if not slow, at least as slow as possible.

Something I needed now.

Voices and footsteps reached me.

'We must hurry,' a man's voice said. 'Wentworth's knowledge of medicine is excellent, but not equal to mine. He will do what he can, but I must return.'

'Oh, please save Adeline,' Tattie squealed, ever the actress. 'I fear she shall die! The baby too!'

It was a risk taking the doctor away from my mother, but I trusted D'Arcy near on as much as I trusted Tattie. He would look after her well, and I needed him occupied.

Tattie burst through the entrance, giving me a glance not noticeable by anyone but us. The doctor and another man followed close behind her, and as soon as they passed by me, I was gone.

And I prayed that the wings Catherine had spoken of found my feet.

***

I sped around the deck, using the knowledge of my previous escapades as well as Tattie's instructions. She had explored the deck often in the last few weeks, making sure she knew every nook and cranny, every twist and turn.

'It was 'ow I survived on the streets, you know,' she'd said to me one night. 'Knowin' 'em better than anyone else. Knowin' where to turn, where to hide, where to sprint and where to walk. When you know that, you can escape anyone.'

And so I ran, wings on my feet, until I reached the orlop deck. Still I didn't stop. I ran on until I again stood where I had stood the night before, looking into the convict area, trying not to avert my eyes, begging for strength.

A crack cut the air, followed by a scream. Mam! I spun, torn, but I knew my part. I knew my priority.

I turned back to the convicts, my eyes finding my father through the dim light.

'Da,' I whispered, my voice hoarse, tentative. He didn't move.

CRACK!

Another scream. That was two. I didn't have time.

'DA!' I called. I knew too much noise could give away my position. I cared not. A few of the men looked up, and my father stirred, but didn't look.

'There,' I said, pointing. 'That man. Thomas O'Hanlon. I must speak to him. Now!'

A convict near my father, bless his soul, reached out and gave my father a gentle shove.

'Da,' I hissed again, and then, praise the Lord, my da, my precious, beautiful da, opened his eyes and looked at me. It took a second, but then his eyes focused and he grinned.

'Oh, do I have stories to tell you, Molly O'Hanlon,' he said, his voice barely reaching me, but when it did it filled my heart.

CRACK!

'Da,' I said. 'I miss you. I miss you so much.'

'I miss you too, sweetheart,' he said. 'But you must stay your distance.'

'I know, Da,' I said. 'I had to see you. I'm so sorry. I had to see you.'

'Your letter,' he said. 'Your letter painted a picture of you in my mind. It is a picture no amount of pain or hunger can erase. You are always with me, Molly O'Hanlon. Always. And I shall always be with you. No matter what.'

CRACK!

That was ten. That was the arranged time. I had to leave.

But I couldn't. I knew the crowd would remain after the fifteenth strike, and that Tattie would keep the doctor until then also.

And I could see my father weakening.

I needed just one more moment.

'Da,' I said. 'I have to go, but I love you. I love you more than anything in the whole entire world.'

He grunted as he shifted his body a little, making me wince, but then he was back. For a second, through the pain, the illness, the hunger, he was back.

'Don't tell your mam that,' he said, and I could see the twinkle in his eye from a mile away. 'Don't you tell her I'm your favourite.'

He closed his eyes then.

'Ah, I'm Molly's favourite,' he said. 'Molly's favourite.'

CRACK!

'Goodbye, Da,' I whispered, and then I turned and ran.

Voices rang out from the whipping post.

'Give 'er one more!'

'She ain't screamed enough!'

I cursed them. I cursed them all, and I longed to run to them, to scream at them, to nurse my mother.

But I would be of no use to her then, and I knew D'Arcy was there.

The best thing I could do was to get back to the women's quarters. I had seen my father. That was enough.

I sped down the deck.

I had two turns to go.

I took the first, and then, as I neared the second, a man appeared in my path. Lucky Gem. Shock was on both our faces, but he reacted first. A hand shot out and struck me in the stomach, knocking me to the ground.

'Gotcha,' he said. 'You ain't gonna be runnin' round these decks again, ya little mongrel.'

The wind had been knocked out of me, and I could scarcely breathe as I was dragged to my feet. A face moved in close to mine, the breath foul, the words fouler.

'I know you,' he said, sneering. 'And I bet good coin I know where you were just now. Seein' that lost cause of a father of yours. Your mam just felt the cut of fifteen lashes, girl. Now it'll be your turn, and you'll be lucky if it's only fifteen. And guess what else?'

I didn't respond. I was still trying to breathe. Then Lucky Gem grinned.

'I wanted your father to get the rope, but this is good enough. It weren't just the money neither. See, he took your mam from me in the early days. She shoulda been mine. And now, when he dies, I'm plannin' on gettin' her back and marryin' her. That's right. I'll be your da, I will.'

He struck me in the stomach again, and again the wind was taken from me. I gasped for air as he started to walk, dragging me along behind him.

'And now,' he said. 'Let's go see Captain Trail.'

CHAPTER 11: THE ANGEL

My vision blurred as I was dragged along, both from the tears and the pain. I prayed for an angel, and when one came it looked nothing like I had imagined.

I had thought that angels had halos and wings and glowed with an aura of gentleness. This angel, however, was very different.

This angel snuck up behind Lucky Gem as though on air, making not a sound. This angel had dirt on her face, and clothes that hadn't seen their original colour in some time.

This angel was my best friend in the whole world. This angel was Tattie.

She moved in beside me, a finger to her lips. Lucky Gem was focused on walking forwards, mumbling to himself of more lashings to come. Tattie made a noose in a section of rope she held. She silently threw it in front of Lucky Gem, and when he stepped in it, she pulled it tight.

With a cry he fell forward, yet still kept his grip on me. I flew into him as he landed and he tumbled over me, knocking the wind from my body, leaving him flat on his back with me on one side of him and Tattie on the other.

Lucky Gem was far from done however and his hands lunged out, one grabbing me, one grabbing Tattie. He stood up, holding us at arm's length, grinning.

'Even better,' he said, looking at each of us in turn. 'Seems like I got me two lashin's for the price o' one.'

I thought all was lost. It was only when I stared at Tattie in desperation that I saw she had a grin on her face even wider than our captor's. I had no idea why, and then I saw her gnash her teeth together. I stared. She rolled her eyes and did it again. My mind finally went back to our training.

'If someone grabs ya,' Tattie had said. 'There's only one thing to do.'

'Try and get away?' I'd asked. She had laughed and laughed, as usual when my answer was not what she had been expecting.

'Yes, Princess, that's right. I'm sure one as strong as Your Majesty will struggle away from the likes of Captain Trail.'

I shrugged and Tattie had leaned in close.

'You bite, Princess. You bite and bite and bite and bite til you can't bite no more! You got it?'

I got it then, and I got it now. I nodded to Tattie and as one we opened our mouths, twisted our heads, and clamped down on Lucky Gem.

I chomped on his thumb, Tattie getting a good toothy grip between his other thumb and a finger. Lucky Gem howled in pain, but we weren't giving up our grips, holding like dogs on a bone.

Tattie even growled. Lucky Gem shook his hands around and eventually we were thrown free. He glared at us, holding his hands. Tattie got onto all fours and growled again. I thought to do the same but knew it would have nowhere near the effect. She seemed like a rabid dog!

Lucky Gem advanced, knowing me the weaker of the two. This was his first mistake. Tattie launched herself at his back, throwing her arms around his neck. He swung his arms back, trying to grab at her, taking his focus off me. This was his second mistake.

'Lesson two,' Tattie had said, 'is that everythin's a weapon. Every ... single ... thing.'

I looked around, wishing for a pistol, a sword, anything, seeing nothing, until my eyes fell upon a rope laying coiled up on the ground. I picked it up. It was heavier than I had expected, but I swung it in a circle and threw it as hard as I could at Lucky Gem.

He howled once again, and the rope stayed attached to him. I saw why as he turned to me. There had been a metal hook attached to the rope I hadn't seen, which was now embedded in his arm!

He roared and ran at me, but Tattie grabbed one end of the rope. It unraveled, twisted round his legs, tripped him up and his head hit the ship's railing, knocking him unconscious in an instant!

Tattie squealed with delight and hugged me as she jumped up and down.

'Come on,' she said. 'We have to get back.'

'You aren't going anywhere,' a voice said. We spun around. My heart leapt with joy when I saw it was D'Arcy, then dropped just as quickly when I saw the look on his face.

He was furious.

***

'What are you doing out here?' he hissed, stepping forward, keeping his voice low as he gathered us close to him. 'You made me a promise.'

I blushed a deep red, ashamed I had let him down.

'I am so sorry, Mr Wentworth, but I had to see him one last time. I had to.'

D'Arcy sighed and turned me to him.

'You have put yourself at great risk,' he said. 'Tattie and myself too. In saying that, however ...'

He looked around to make sure no one had yet joined us, then looked back at us, a cheeky grin on his face.

'You two have somehow taken down a man twice your size! I want to hear all about it, but not now.'

'Mr Wentworth, what goes?' said a man I recognised as the doctor, who ran up to us. D'Arcy stood.

'Dr. Gray,' he said, striding forward, shielding us and shaking the doctor's hand. 'I'm afraid this man has had a fall and struck his head ... and apparently landed on a metal hook. I have had a quick look at him, but trust you shall give him better care than I.'

The doctor nodded, then looked at Tattie.

'Your friend Adeline is fine,' he said. 'Despite her making the noise of a thousand cats and you dragging me away from my duties, there was nothing wrong with her. Interesting, hmmmmm?'

It seemed like Adeline had done her job of acting as a distraction very well.

Tattie shrugged.

'Good fortune, all round,' she said. 'And now, goodness, but we have chores to carry out in our quarters. We must run!'

Before we went, I turned to D'Arcy.

'Mr Wentworth,' I said. 'Do you think …'

My voice trailed off and I looked at Lucky Gem, wondering whether he would tell of what we had done to him. I was shocked when D'Arcy smiled and led me out of earshot of Dr Gray.

'Molly, I have some experience in courtrooms, and I tell you this. I have known people who avoided giving evidence that may have sent a man to the gallows, and the reason they did not speak out was to protect their own reputation. I don't believe Lucky Gem will be telling anyone two young girls got the better of him, do you?'

I smiled back, more out of relief then joy.

'I would, however,' D'Arcy continued, 'steer clear of him at all costs. He curries good favour with the Captain. You have made an enemy here today. Do not be surprised if he makes up some sort of furphy to tell Captain Trail. Lay low, Molly, and this time I need your promise to be true.'

I nodded and promised. I was tempted to tell D'Arcy what Lucky Gem had said about my parents, my mother in particular, for it didn't make sense to me. But something told me I had pushed my luck far enough for one day, and not to push it any further.

So I thanked him, I took Tattie's hand, and we returned to our quarters.

***

We didn't have much time to celebrate our victory over Lucky Gem however, for when we returned my mother was already there. She lay on her side on the bunk and looked at me sadly.

'Mam!' I cried, forgetting myself and running to embrace her. She gasped when I did so, but still held me close, her tears starting to flow.

I suddenly remembered and released her.

'Your back!' I cried. 'Mam, your back. I'm so sorry.'

She smiled at me.

'Molly, I would take a thousand lashes and still wish to be hugged by you, my brave girl. You too, Tattie. Margaret and the others have told me of what you did today. I can't even find the words.'

She sniffed, tears appearing in her eyes. I sat next to her, very carefully putting an arm around her.

'They're two brave girls, alright,' Margaret said. 'Though I must admit, the time since they left to now has been time my heart barely beat. I thought you two thrown overboard.'

'We almost were!' Tattie cried, before relating our tale to the others in very exaggerated) detail. Tattie was in her element, acting out the fight, playing the part of herself, me and even Lucky Gem, bringing howls of laughter from the women.

But only one reaction mattered to me ... the pride on my mother's face.

'And your father?' she asked. 'What of him, Molly?'

I looked at her.

'He is not well, Mam. But for an instant his eye held a twinkle, and in that instant he felt alive to me.'

'That's good, Molly. That is very, very good.'

She closed her eyes and lay on her side, sighing.

'I must rest now. I'm very proud of both of you girls.'

I lay in front of her, also on my side, and let her hold me, but we had only settled in for a short time when D'Arcy appeared at the door with Dr Gray. D'Arcy stayed at the entrance while Dr Gray entered and came to my mother.

I lay with Mam and let her hold me.

'Your wounds?' he asked.

She nodded.

'Good enough,' she replied, before wincing to show her words covered up the truth.

'Very well,' he said, his eyes holding a deep sadness. 'And there is good news. You did not contract the illness your husband had.'

I grinned, but noticed the sadness remained in his eyes.

'What is it?' I asked.

'I'm here to bring sad news, I am afraid. It is your husband. He ...'

He didn't finish the sentence. He didn't need to. We all knew the what was to come. I started to cry.

'Come now, Molly,' Mam said, holding me close. 'We must remember the good times we had with your father. We must be strong now. He would want that. He would want us to tell tales of him to others, to help him live on.'

I nodded, but the tears wouldn't stop. Dr Gray suddenly leaned in very close.

'We should not let you do this,' he said, 'but the

risks you have both taken tell me as much about the man Thomas was as they do about the women you are. All other convicts who passed have been unceremoniously dumped overboard with no one to mourn them. I don't believe Thomas is deserving of that fate. We are to bury him at sea after dark. Tonight. We will find a way for you to be there to say goodbye … if you can manage it.'

Mam did cry then, her strength fading at this kindest of gestures.

'You *must* go,' Margaret said. The other women chorused their agreement.

'We'll do whatever we 'ave to,' Tattie said. 'Ain't no way they'll know you was even gone.'

'Thank you, Tattie,' Mam said. 'Thank you everyone, and thank you, Dr Gray. We would like that very, very much. But I must rest first.'

'Of course,' Dr Gray said, rising and walking to the door. 'We shall come for you when it is time.'

I looked at D'Arcy, who had stayed at the door the whole time. He nodded to me, and I returned the nod, and then he and Dr Gray were gone.

Gone. Just like my father was. Although unlike my father, D'Arcy would once again return when I was in need.

CHAPTER 12: THE BURIAL

That next night was one of the saddest, hardest and yet proudest of my short life.

As I walked with Mam along the deck, guided by Tattie, of course, I felt as if I was in a dream. It was real, yet it also felt like it was unreal. Almost like I was watching these things happen to someone else.

Even Tattie held her tongue, and we walked in silence. I had my arm around my mother, careful to avoid the areas the lash had struck, which was most of her back. I cursed myself over and again for screaming, for being the reason she had been caught at all and swore I would not make a sound on this occasion, no matter what.

Mam was still very poorly and needed support as she walked, hence my arm around her waist, holding her steady, but also giving me great comfort, knowing that while I had lost one parent, the other was as close to me as she could ever be.

We reached the orlop deck without incident and met with D'Arcy and Dr Gray who were waiting there for us. D'Arcy took my mother's hand and bowed his head. Dr Gray did the same.

I looked into the men's quarters and saw them there, all shackled, but all watching us.

'Your pappy,' one said. 'He was a fine man. I knew him only this short time, but already he made me feel more of a man meself.'

There was a chorus of agreement from some of the others.

'He told us stories, he did,' said another. 'Every night, no matter how sick he felt, and I can tell ye he felt mighty sick a lot of the time. But still he told us stories.'

Again, the others chorused their agreement. And so it went on. Different men each time, all telling a short sentence of how my father had touched them while they lay there, sick, dying, locked in.

How he had lifted their spirits every day.

And how he had talked every single day, *every single day*, about me and Mam. He had talked of his love for us, and had memorised my letter and said it out loud every night before he slept, and how it felt, to all of them, as though they themselves had received a letter from their loved ones.

'Thank you, girlie,' said a man. 'Your letter 'elped us through many a long night, it did.'

I had held back tears until then, but I could hold back no longer, and they flowed freely down my cheeks.

Mam squeezed my shoulder and Tattie squeezed my hand, and then, though their hands weren't free, the convicts that could started to rattle the chains that held them, quietly but firmly, softly but with passion, as my father was carried out by two crew the doctor trusted.

'I was right,' Dr Gray said as his voice cracked. 'A fine man. A fine man indeed.'

'Step back now, Molly,' D'Arcy said gently. I did as he bade, and watched as my father was carried past, too far away to touch but close enough for me to want to reach out.

I wanted more than anything to touch my father's hand one last time. But Dr Gray told us that would be dangerous. We were still liable to contract the illness he had if we were too close. The men who carried him wore rags over their mouths, but we did not have those at hand, and besides, as much as I yearned to reach out, to touch my father when he had no life felt as though I would be touching a ghost, and I didn't wish to do that ever.

So I silently cried, and I watched as the men carried him to the edge of the ship.

'Goodbye, Thomas,' Mam whispered, holding me a little tighter.

'Goodbye, Da,' I said just as quietly, but I knew

he heard us both. Wherever he was, he heard us both, I was as sure of it as I had ever been sure of anything.

'Bye, Molly's dad,' Tattie said. 'If she's a Princess, that means you must have been a King.'

I looked at her to see if she was joking, but her eyes were wet with tears and she stared straight at my father, nothing but respect on her face. I let go of my mother and turned to Tattie, holding her close. She was my best friend. She was my rock.

'Thank you, Tattie,' I said, and then we held each other as D'Arcy said a few quiet words, and then my father was thrown over the ship's railings, landing with a splash that sent a jolt through me.

It was final now.

He was gone.

***

I couldn't sleep after that. All I could hear was that splash, that final splash, over and over again.

'Mam?' I whispered after a time. She didn't answer immediately, and when she sniffed I realised I had interrupted her tears.

'Yes, Molly,' she said, a tremor in her voice.

'Mam, I can't sleep,' I said. 'I ...'

My voice trailed off and then, before I knew it, Mam was behind me, lying on my bunk, holding me.

'I know, Molly. I know,' she said.

We lay there for a while after that, neither of us sleeping, and then, from nowhere, my mam started to quietly sing to me, a song her and Da sang every year as I celebrated my birthday.

It was my song.

There was a girl called Molly, she was so very small,
But every time we looked at her, well we felt eight foot tall.
When she was just a baby, she screamed and screamed so loud,
She does that sometimes still but Molly, you make us so proud.'

And on she sang, stroking my hair, holding me, and in her voice I heard my da singing as well, and before I knew it, I had drifted off to sleep, a smile on my tear-stained face.

***

The weeks after that were not good. Mam was confined to her bed, and I spent most of my time with her, unable even to play games with Tattie.

The reason for this was the lashes my mother had received. Despite the care of Dr Gray, spending time of his own to check on her, the wounds became infected, and looked harsher and redder as time passed.

'I don't understand it,' Dr Gray said to D'Arcy on one occasion, both unaware I was listening in, using skills learned from Tattie to be unnoticed.

'She should be healing,' Dr Gray continued. 'It sometimes happens when the wounds get infected, but usually this is because the person doesn't receive the proper care. There is nothing else I can do, and yet still the wounds fester. If it continues ...'

His voice trailed off then, and I saw D'Arcy lay a hand on his shoulder.

'You are doing all you can,' he said, 'and I implore you to continue to do so. The girl has lost one parent. I do not know what it would do to her to lose another, and so swiftly after.'

I left then, not wanting to hear anymore. They were cuts from a lash, how could that lead to my mother's death? I laughed to myself. Dr Gray and D'Arcy believed themselves smart, smarter than most even, and yet they were making such an amateur blunder in this case.

I sat on my mother's bunk and smiled, a smile she returned as I gently brushed a stray strand of hair off her face. This felt odd to me. It was usually Mam taking care of me, yet now it seemed we had changed roles.

See? A smile. She was and would always be fine. She would heal, the infection would be gone, and we would spend the rest of the voyage together, laughing with Tattie, talking with D'Arcy, and thinking of a time long past when she had been ill.

***

'We have a month to go, Molly,' D'Arcy said to me one day. 'A month and we shall be docking at False Bay just outside of Cape Town.'

False Bay - it was a name that seemed appropriate, given the false accusations against my father and the reason we were on this ship in the first place.

'Are you sure?' I joked. 'Is it true, or is it a trick?'

D'Arcy laughed out loud, shocking me. He was usually so restrained. It was a wonderful sound though, and I soon joined in, giggling as I covered my hand. Eventually he stopped and sighed.

'Oh Molly, I have yet to meet one so brave and positive as you,' he said, before shaking his head, as if to refocus. 'When we reach our destination, I am to leave the boat. I would like you to come with me,' he said. 'Molly, your mother is worsening by the day.'

'No, Mr Wentworth,' I cut in. 'I see her every day, and you do not. Dr Gray neither. You do not see the little signs, the little improvements. I am sure by the time we reach this Cape Town, she will be fine.'

D'Arcy went to speak, thought better of it, and then started again.

'Perhaps you are right, Molly,' he said, although his eyes betrayed his words. 'Perhaps by Cape Town your mother shall be able to come with us. If she cannot, however, we must get medical supplies. Dr Gray is required to stay on board, so I have told Captain Trail you are my assistant in such matters and will help to carry these supplies back to the ship. Some of them will be for the crew, and some will be for your mother. Those are the ones you will bring.'

I nodded.

'Can I go back to Mam now?' I asked, my voice quiet. D'Arcy nodded.

'Yes, Molly, and you give her my best. Make sure to call for me if she … well, if things take a turn from the positive direction they currently travel.'

He patted my shoulder and left, and I ran to my mother's bunk, sitting immediately and holding her hand. Despite my strong words, and despite my belief my mother would get better, had to get better, I knew the truth.

I knew, in my heart, that I was not being honest with myself. I feared my mother would not last the voyage, for she had indeed worsened in the last weeks. But to say it out loud seemed as if it would make it truer, and so I couldn't admit to it.

I couldn't.

And so, for selfish reasons alone, when Mam thrashed about that night in her sleep, when her fever worsened, when she cried out words I cannot repeat, I did nothing but lie with her and hold her.

I did the same the following nights as well, always believing she would get past it and be okay.

And in doing so, I may well have written her death sentence.

***

When the morning came that my mother didn't wake, I couldn't be consoled. I had kept my silence when hearing of my father's end, and had tried to stay strong, but this time I couldn't. I didn't have it in me.

All my strength had been drawn from my body, from my soul, and I wailed, I shook her lifeless body, and I screamed and I cried and I scratched myself on the arm, and I wouldn't let Tattie or Margaret or anyone pull me away.

I begged her to return to me, I begged her with everything I had left, and of that there was not much.

I held her, and I tried to pour my heart into hers. I breathed into her mouth and I screamed in frustration, railing at the evil ship we had boarded, the ship that had killed my parents, and I swore revenge on Lucky Gem, I swore it to all who would listen. I swore that man would not get away with what he had done.

I pressed on my mother's chest, I pressed and pressed, and I tore the locket from her neck, desperate to have something of hers on me, always. It was the locket she wore at all times. My father had given to her, with a picture of me inside it.

It was only when D'Arcy's strong hands took hold of me that I was pulled away, and even then it was with kicking legs and thrashing arms, but he held firm, and he held me close, whispering how sorry he was, whispering how I would be okay, he would make sure I was okay, and to hush now, to quieten, to speak not of Lucky Gem or the *Neptune*, to leave those words for another time when ears that shouldn't hear such things may not be listening.

And he held me as they took my mother away. D'Arcy asked if I wished to see her burial as well, her burial at sea, but I shook my head and cried again.

I couldn't bear it. I couldn't say goodbye to me mam like I had with me da. I couldn't do it, because to say goodbye to her like that, to see her body thrown overboard, that would make it final, and I couldn't do that.

Not yet.

I couldn't say it because that would mean she was gone forever, and now, more than ever before, I needed the one thing I would never have again.

I needed my mam.

CHAPTER 13: THE ARRIVAL

Weeks later I saw land before most, as I spent most of my days outside the women's quarters, staring over the railing. I cared not that I wasn't meant to be outside, and that I may get into trouble. It seemed none of the crew cared either, for they walked past me without a word on most occasions.

Only Lucky Gem, despite, or perhaps because of, his knowledge of my mother's death, of both my parents' deaths, still found cause to have words as he passed.

'You killed them both, you know,' was one of his favourites. 'You ruined my chances, so I will take away yours,' was another.

Most of the time the words were just a sound on the wind and were easily ignored. On other occasions though, I not only heard the words but felt them too, for although I blamed Lucky Gem for both my parents' deaths, still I knew I was at fault too.

It was at these times I would clutch the locket I had taken from Mam, I would hold it till it dug into my palm, and I would think of her, and Da too, and I would feel their strength fill me.

D'Arcy had checked in on me often. He had even offered for me to stay on a small bunk in his cabin, but I declined.

It was an easy choice.

Partly, it didn't feel right to accept, but mostly it was because I needed to be in the space where Mam had been with me. I needed to be around her memory. And so I slept in her bunk from the day she passed.

D'Arcy accepted my decision, but also informed me he had asked Catherine to keep an eye on me, and to inform him of any troubles I may have. I was grateful for this, but it did also make me feel like a little girl.

Tattie tried to convince me none of what had happened was my fault, but even she had given up when it was clear the burden was too heavy for her to lift from my heart. So she sat with me on deck, saying little, doing less.

Until suddenly she leapt to her feet and pointed.

'Land!' she said breathlessly. 'I see land, I do!'

I leapt up as well, my body betraying my heart, and I stared. Land. We had seen none of it for so long, and now here we were, staring at a speck on the horizon that signified something other than the endless sea. It suddenly made us feel so alive!

I moaned out loud without meaning to, the word *alive* enough to bring everything crashing back down on me. Tattie dashed to my side and held me, but I shook my head.

'I'm okay,' I said, my voice croaky with the first words I had spoken in weeks. Tattie gasped.

'It speaks!' she said, shock all over her face. 'It has risen from the depths and spoken, though it ain't a pleasant voice to hear. Oh, mercy me.'

Then she put the back of her hand to her forehead and mimed a faint, forcing me to jump in and catch her, though being all of eleven with, as mentioned all those months ago when we were on the docks, very weak arms, I caught nothing and we crashed to the deck.

'Don't,' I said, pointing a finger at Tattie. 'Don't you laugh!'

Tattie bit her cheeks, her eyes worried with strain, and her body tensed to bursting.

'Oh, for heaven's sakes, Tattie, why do you do this to me?' I groaned, and Tattie burst out laughing, knowing I was done as well. I didn't laugh with her, I wasn't ready for that, not yet, but I did smile. Tattie saw and hugged me close.

'You will get through this, Molly O'Hanlon,' she whispered in my ear. I shook my head, the tears rising again.

'How?' I asked. 'I don't know how, Tattie.'

'Because you're strong, and brave, and you 'ave me, Princess,' she said, before giving me another squeeze and standing. 'Now get ready. I got me an announcement to make.'

She ran off, screaming at the top of her lungs.

'Land!' she screamed. 'Land, and I saw it first, I did!'

All the women ran out from our quarters to look, as did most of the crew, staring and pointing.

After three long months at sea, we had reached False Bay and the magical city of Cape Town.

***

I watched as people prepared to go from our ship and onto land. I also saw others disembarking from the *Scarborough* and *Surprize*, two other ships which were part of the Second Fleet. Among those leaving the *Scarborough* for the shore was, to my surprise, Mr Macarthur, he of the duel.

He looked to our ship as his landing boat passed, and it was not a happy glance. However, when he saw some of us girls watching, he smiled and waved, and we waved in reply.

On our deck, Lucky Gem stood by Captain Trail,

parchment in hand. I shook my head, my disgust at him clouding my memory so much that I had forgotten to tell D'Arcy of the plot cooked up between Captain Trail and Lucky Gem.

Some other government officials also went ashore, most with their families.

I would not be one of those to go, I assumed. D'Arcy had said I could, but only to get medical supplies for my mother, and now ... well, they were not needed anymore.

'Where is that cursed Wentworth?' fumed Captain Trail. 'Anchors are down, ropes are tied, and we are due to go ashore at once. He has -'

'My apologies, Captain Trail,' D'Arcy said, walking briskly over the deck towards the gangplank. 'I was in deep discussion with Dr Gray.'

'What of it, Wentworth?' the Captain asked. 'What do I care of your conversations?'

D'Arcy glanced at me then smiled innocently at the captain, who glowered back in return.

'It seems,' D'Arcy said, 'that Dr Gray is in need of medical supplies, more than I shall be able to carry. Therefore, I have selected Miss Molly O'Hanlon to be my assistant in this case. She shall come ashore and help ease the load.'

'A child?' burst out Lucky Gem, glaring at me. 'And a child who is apt to break rules at every turn, no less?'

I almost laughed at that, seeing as he was one to break more laws than I even knew of.

'Quiet,' Captain Trail ordered. 'The girl shall come, this is of no concern to me. But she is your concern, Wentworth, and if anything happens, or if she does not make it back on board before we set sail, be it on your head.'

A chill went down my spine. That had seemed more a threat than advice. The tension in the air was soon lessened though.

'And a fine head it is, too,' said Catherine from the entrance to our quarters. This sent the women into fits of laughter and forced Captain Trail to send two crewmen to silence them.

'We board the longboats now,' he said, turning and barking orders to the crew. D'Arcy bent down to my level as people started to leave the *Neptune's* deck, returning to their quarters or heading ashore.

'Why?' I asked. 'I was only to go ashore to help my mother, and …'

D'Arcy smiled, then moved his hands from behind his back and held out a parasol to me.

'It's beautiful,' I breathed, taking it. 'Where did you get it?'

'The where is of no concern, Molly. The why, however, is. You have had a hard voyage so far, harder than anyone should experience, let alone a young girl. But you have weathered storms that would destroy others.'

'I feel destroyed inside, Mr Wentworth,' I said, averting my eyes and holding out the parasol, not feeling worthy of it anymore. But he gently returned my arm to my side.

'Molly,' he said, 'if you did not feel an intense amount of pain right now, you would not be human. To be able to rise each morning shows you are a human of rare quality, someone your parents would be most proud of.'

I looked at him.

'Really?' I asked, my voice barely a whisper.

He nodded.

'Most definitely really,' he said. 'You deserve to disembark with me, for Cape Town holds wonders from afar that I am excited to see. Oh, I believe this will be a fine distraction from your hardships, Molly.'

'What shall we see?' I asked.

'Never mind that,' he said. 'You shall find out soon enough. Come on, Molly, raise your parasol. You are about to enter Cape Town, the oldest city in the region. And guess what?'

'What?' I asked as I held my parasol above my head, feeling quite the lady.

'It is known as the Mother City. Everywhere we go, Molly, there will be signs your mother is watching over you. This is just the first.'

And with that, D'Arcy helped me into one of the longboats, and we headed for shore. We were soon on dry land and then, under the shadows of a huge rock known as Table Mountain, we made our way north to Cape Town.

***

D'Arcy was wrong. The sights didn't overwhelm me. The sights and the sounds and the smells overwhelmed me. It was … no, words can barely do it justice. Suffice to say I saw buildings the likes of which my hometown would never see.

'The Garden House,' D'Arcy said, pointing at a building which was amazing in both size and beauty. 'It has only recently been rebuilt.'

'Who built it?' I asked, staring.

'Slaves, Molly,' D'Arcy said softly. 'It is a tradition I pray ends soon, but one that currently provides the wealthy with free labour. If you ever, ever encounter a slave, Molly, I beg of you, treat them well. Treat them as though they were a king or queen, and you will be rewarded not only with their loyalty, but with a place reserved for you in the heavens above.'

I nodded, my eyes wide. I had heard of slavery before but had never seen evidence of it.

'Come now,' D'Arcy said. 'While extremely important, that is all a bit glum, and something we shall rectify when we can. Let us explore the Castle of Good Hope and see the interior these fine men and women helped construct.'

'Why is it called Good Hope?' I asked.

'An excellent question, Molly. Remember this, if you want excellent answers, ask excellent questions. This whole area,' he said, waving an arm, 'is known as the Cape of Good Hope.'

'I thought we were in Cape Town.'

'And that we are, however Cape Town is just one part of the Cape. This, where we are now, is the opening of a new trade route to the east, one that will open up the world's potential. At least,' and at this he winked at me, 'that is what we … hope.'

I giggled. D'Arcy was always able to infuse his lessons with some humour, something I would always be grateful to him for. We reached the castle, another building amazing in its magnificence.

'How are we permitted inside?' I asked D'Arcy.

He winked once again.

'Sometimes, Molly O'Hanlon, being able to converse with all manner of men is a worthy skill. As is knowing what they desire.'

And that was all he would say on the topic, so I let it go and enjoyed the sights that lay inside the castle.

But the sight that gave me the biggest thrill, one that I will remember for my entire life, was Greenmarket Square. Oh, if I close my eyes, even at this distance of time from that day, I can smell Greenmarket Square. Foods, spices, animals, fresh meats and vegetables.

And I can hear the stallholders crying out, telling all of their wares, many of them speaking in words I could not understand.

'But how do we understand them?' I asked D'Arcy. 'Some of them speak words that make no sense.'

'What you are experiencing, Molly, is the world in one place. Where do you hail from?'

'Ireland,' I said. 'As do you. You know that.'

'I do,' D'Arcy laughed, 'and a fine land it is. But these people, this place, it's different. Cape Town, is midway between many lands, so is a stopping point for all nationalities. Some hail from Asia, some from Europe, some from the Americas, and some, of course, like you and I, from Ireland and England.'

I couldn't believe it. I had always assumed all people looked like me and my parents, or the women and men aboard the *Neptune*, but Greenmarket Square opened my eyes for the first time. People didn't look alike, or sound alike, and yet D'Arcy treated them all with the same respect, care and manners that he would have treated the King himself.

I watched him that day, and from that point on, as this was teaching in its finest form - showing, and not telling. I had learnt from Tattie, and she from me, yet D'Arcy would become my greatest teacher, both in his words and deeds.

I was in awe of him, how he could make someone laugh and feel at ease, even if he spoke not their language.

He was amazing, but the animals we saw were even more so.

'What's that one?' I asked, pointing.

'A tiger,' D'Arcy replied. 'The largest of all land cats, and extremely intelligent. Do you know, it can imitate other animals?'

I gasped.

'Could it imitate me?'

D'Arcy laughed, and went to speak, but I beat him to it.

'That one!' I squealed, all manners forgotten. 'What's that one?'

'A monkey, Molly. They're cheeky, just like you!'

I feigned offence.

'Humph,' I said. 'Tattie maybe, but never me!'

On and on it went, the animals, the people, and the food, oh the food!

Foods unlike any I had ever eaten, with flavours and aromas that sent me to other lands. I only stopped eating when D'Arcy reminded me we needed to collect medical supplies, and so off we went.

D'Arcy had said there would be a place reserved for me in heaven, but it felt like I was already there.

I never wanted the day to end.

Visiting Greenmarket Square in Cape Town.

CHAPTER 14: THE BANQUET

My wish for the day to never end continued into my wish for the time to never end. For two whole weeks, D'Arcy and I walked the streets of Cape Town to collect supplies. Most of the time was spent with me staring and asking questions, him answering them and filling my brain with facts and wonder.

Was he right every time? I had to assume so, but a large part of me cared not if he was right or wrong, for every piece of information was so wonderful.

Each night saw us returning to the *Neptune*, and I would relay the day's experiences and lessons to Tattie, and sometimes the others in our lodgings as well. I noticed Catherine would often listen in, and I assumed she was curious as to Cape Town's delights. I also liked entertaining the woman who had been asked to make sure I was okay.

All of this made me feel so much older than my eleven years, although as I pointed out to Tattie, my twelfth birthday was not far off. Unfortunately, mentioning that brought me to tears, as I realised it would be my first birthday without my mother's cake, or my father's stories and terrible singing that always made me laugh.

Tattie held me and turned to the others.

'Oi! You lot! This 'ere young lady will soon reach the

grand age of twelve. She's near on a lady, she is. We won't let it go by without a celebration, will we?'

'No!' chorused the women. Margaret came over.

'Just because your parents are no longer with us doesn't mean you don't have a family,' she said, bringing on more tears. I tried to wipe them away, but Margaret stopped me.

'No,' she said. 'Let them flow. Every tear is a way of holding onto a memory. So never hold back the tears, or the memories shall fade.'

I nodded and turned to Tattie.

'Tomorrow is my final day in Cape Town,' I said. 'We set sail the following day. You remember what Mr Wentworth gave us for our shoe shining?'

Tattie shook her head.

'No,' she said. 'I only remember that he saved us from most likely bein' thrown overboard.'

I smiled, reached into my tunic, and pulled out the shiny coin we had received.

'I have seen so many things I should like to purchase,' I said, 'but I need your help. Tell me, Tattie. Is there anything you would like me to bring back for you? For us?'

Tattie leapt off the bed, swirling in circles.

'Oh my,' she said, putting on a posh English accent. 'Why, with this kind of fortune, I want the world! Say, can you bring me one of those tiger creatures? That would be fun to play with and to let eat Lucky Gem.'

She swirled some more until she collapsed on the bed, and my tears of sorrow mixed with tears of laughter. Tattie sat up straight with a gasp.

'Molly,' she said, suddenly serious. 'Can you bring me some food, somethin' I would never 'ave eaten before, somethin' I would never see back 'ome.'

I nodded. I had no idea what I would bring, but I knew it was going to be special.

***

The following day, as we walked through Greenmarket Square towards the *Neptune*, my arms filled with supplies, I suddenly remembered my promise to Tattie.

'Mr Wentworth!' I gasped. 'I promised Tattie I would get her something special to eat from a market stall, something wondrous she would never before have tried.'

D'Arcy looked at my full arms and smiled.

'How much longer do you believe your arms can last till you must put those down?' he asked.

I thought about it. My arms were burning, but I tried never to show it. Perhaps I could run back to the ship then return, or perhaps I could carry these supplies while I searched for a treat for Tattie.

D'Arcy interrupted my thoughts.

'Well, it seems like you are fine, for it has been a good few minutes since I even asked the question.'

'Sorry, Mr Wentworth,' I said. 'It's just, I fear if I return to the ship with these I shan't be let back out again.'

'But Molly,' he replied, feigning shock. 'If you return to the ship and do not come back to Cape Town, how can you possibly attend the dinner the Dutch Governor is holding tonight? The dinner that only the most special of all people are invited to, including Captain Trail, Mr Macarthur, one D'Arcy Wentworth and, of course ...'

He produced an invitation with a flourish, an invitation baring my name.

'My assistant, Miss Molly O'Hanlon.'

I gasped and near on dropped everything I was carrying. I was speechless. D'Arcy smiled.

'Come Molly, let us take these to Dr Gray and then return to the Greenmarket Square. On doing so, we shall purchase something for your friend, and also an outfit for you to wear to the dinner tonight.'

'New clothes?' I asked. 'Do you mock me, Mr Wentworth?'

He shook his head.

'No, Molly. This is a very special occasion, and as I mentioned earlier, you are a very special girl who has endured so much. This is an early birthday present from myself to you.'

'How did you know?' I asked. 'I have told no one.'

'You told Tattie,' D'Arcy smiled, 'and so you might as well have told me.'

I grinned, and we walked back to the ship.

From the depths of despair, I was starting to see some light and a way forward.

I prayed that would continue for a long time yet.

***

'Oh my!' Tattie squealed as I walked up and down between the bunks in my new outfit. 'You do look like a real Princess, Molly O'Hanlon.'

She tore off another piece of bread and dipped it in the bowl of stew I had purchased from an African stall and shoved the bread in her mouth. In nearly the same motion, she swept up the jars of Asian spices and breathed in their aroma.

'Tell me again,' she said, her mouth full of stew. 'Do I eat these or just sniff 'em?'

I laughed, her joy overwhelming any manners.

'Both,' I said, 'but D'Arcy mentioned the spices go **INTO** the food.'

'Never!' cried Tattie, bits of stew flying out of her mouth. 'I ain't never wastin' these 'ere smells, ever!'

There was a knock at the door. We all turned and saw it was D'Arcy. I felt rather than saw Catherine move to my side.

'Ain't she look pretty, Mr Wentworth?' she said in that quiet voice of hers.

'She certainly does, Catherine,' D'Arcy said, smiling. 'Come now, Molly, it's time for us to experience something we may never see again.'

'It won't be better than these things Molly got me,' Tattie said, grinning to show the bits of food between her teeth. 'Nothin' in the world could be better 'n' this.'

I hugged her goodbye and then left with D'Arcy. I had no idea what we were walking into.

If I had known, I may have stayed on the ship that night.

***

We were being hosted, as D'Arcy had said, by the Dutch Governor, and we were being hosted in the Garden House. As magnificent as it had looked on the outside, that was nothing compared to the way it looked on the inside for the formal dinner.

I had never seen the likes of it before, and never would again.

Gold seemed to gleam from everywhere, on walls, frames of paintings, the candelabras, everywhere. The colours and the lighting and the smells were all simply amazing.

'It's wonderful, Mr Wentworth,' I said. 'They must be wonderful people to have such a place.'

D'Arcy sighed.

'I wish it were so, Molly, but unfortunately it is not always the case that a person's values and morals match their income. Those with the most money are not always the nicest of people. Yes, this is a wonderful place, but never forget who built it.'

'The slaves?' I asked quietly. He nodded.

'Correct, and while I have heard treatment of them here was not the worst, still it was not the best either. But this is a rather depressing topic to begin such a wonderful evening. Molly, promise me this. Always enjoy yourself, but never forget where you came from, and never forget that an excess of money does not always equal an excess of goodness. Promise?'

'Yes, Mr Wentworth.'

'Good, then let us see what delights are in store for us.'

And so we entered the dining area, and I was amazed anew. Even more valuables glittered, both in the design of the room and on the bodies of the people attending. I had never seen so many jewels, and I was particularly fascinated by a gold candlestick on a mantle.

It was the most beautiful thing I had ever seen, and I knew my parents would have delighted in it as well.

'You keep your grubby 'ands off it,' a gravelly voice hissed in my ear, making me jump. I spun around. D'Arcy was engaged in conversation with a man and a woman, and the voice belonged to Lucky Gem.

'You shouldn't be 'ere,' he said, leaning in close, his breath foul. 'I see you doin' anythin' you shouldn't, I'll be tellin' the captain I will. You'll be back on the ship and in chains like your father was, y'hear?'

I nodded, terrified, then walked briskly off.

'Ta-ra, you little brat,' Lucky Gem hissed as I left.

I quickly made my way to D'Arcy, who immediately noticed something was off.

'Are you okay?' he asked. I nodded, worried if I spoke the tears would come. D'Arcy knew all was not well, but he took me by the arm to our place at the table, and it wasn't long before the tastes and smells overrode my fear of Lucky Gem.

It was a wonderful night from then on, D'Arcy never leaving my side, introducing me to so many other wonderful people my head spun.

As amazing as it was though, my eyes began to feel heavy, and my feet ached.

'Is it time for us to return to the *Neptune*?' D'Arcy asked. I closed my eyes and shook my head, determined not to be the reason this evening came to an end.

Unfortunately, it was harder to open my eyes than I had imagined, and with a laugh, D'Arcy helped me to my feet from the comfortable couch I sat on.

'Come, Molly. Our night is at an end. Let us farewell our hosts and return to our bunks to dream of this wonderful time. Tomorrow, we sail again.'

I nodded, my eyes feeling like lead, and I didn't even realise I had fallen asleep until I was being placed in my bunk by D'Arcy.

It was the best of times.

CHAPTER 15: THE ACCUSATION

The next morning saw us ready to depart. It was April 29th, 1790, and it would be another two months at sea before we would see land again.

And that was only if all was well on the journey.

But the skies were clear, my belly was full, and though the memory of my parents still haunted me, it felt like there had been a change in the air.

Tattie and I watched as twelve new convicts boarded the *Neptune*. These were convicts who had been stranded in Cape Town when their ship, the *Guardian*, sank months earlier

'It's a crime, that is,' Tattie said. 'Takin' up even more space.'

'It matters not,' I replied. 'Mr Wentworth informed me that many convicts have already died, so there is space to bring on more.'

Tattie scoffed and turned away, disgusted.

'If I got me 'ands on that Captain Trail, I reckon I'd wring 'is scrawny neck, I would,' she said, showing me exactly how she'd do it, pulling a face so determined it made me smile.

'Tattie,' I said, 'I saw Captain Trail last night, at the

dinner. He was well behaved. Maybe he's changed and will be a fairer man. Even so, perhaps it's to continue to stay away from him as much as we can.'

'Oh,' Tattie said. 'I'm sure the good Captain was 'is best self last night, around all them fancy people. Trust me, Princess, that was for show, that was. 'E'll be back to 'is demon self soon as we depart.'

'WHAT?' came a roar from on deck. We raced to the deck to see what was happening. It was Captain Trail, talking to a man I recognised from the night before, a messenger of the Governor. The captain turned and glared, and when he saw us, his face darkened further.

We ducked away, staying hidden while others rushed to see what the commotion was about.

It seemed an age before Captain Trail spoke again. He climbed onto the upper deck and glared at the assembled people.

'An extremely valuable item was stolen from the Governor's residence last night. It seems suspicion has fallen upon this ship, **my** ship. It shall be searched, top to bottom. If found, the guilty party shall feel my wrath.'

With that he stepped aside, and members of the Governor's private guard moved past him. Captain Trail stopped them as he caught sight of me.

'Begin with the women's quarters,' he said. 'One of them was admiring the object in question.'

I gasped. He was looking at me? But why? Surely he knew I was with D'Arcy the whole time.

Tattie grabbed my arm and I ran with her.

'You didn't take nothin',' she said, and it wasn't a question. I breathed easier at her undying faith in me, and I nodded.

'No,' I said as we reached my bunk. 'I know not what the object even is.'

'Think, Molly,' Tattie urged. 'Think what you was lookin' at.'

I thought. I had looked at everything! Then, as the smell washed over the ship from the docks, I remembered.

I remembered Lucky Gem's foul breath.

'The gold candlestick,' I breathed. 'It was so pretty. I admired it while on my own, when Mr Wentworth was talking to others. As I did so, Lucky Gem spoke to me, warning me not to take it. It was him, Tattie. I *know* it was! It *has* to be!'

Before she could answer, the Governor's guards stood at our door and we were all ordered to leave.

After that, they proceeded to turn everything upside down in search of the missing gold candlestick.

***

They found, of course, nothing. Not in our lodgings and, it turned out, not anywhere else on-board.

A red-faced Captain Trail, informed the guards, and in turn the Governor, that he would be sure to find it if it was on board, and that they would return it when next they made port at Cape Town.

The Governor was satisfied with this, but the Captain nowhere near so. He fumed as we departed, and it was only when we were clear of Cape Town that he gathered together all those who had attended the dinner.

'I suspect Macarthur,' boomed Captain Trail as we stood in front of him. 'Though he travels on the *Scarborough*, he was the reason Captain Gilbert was removed from duty. It would surprise me not if he was the culprit here, and placed blame on the *Neptune* to cause embarrassment to the Second Fleet.'

I scoffed to myself. This said by a man responsible for the deaths of convicts, including my father, and he was worried about someone else embarrassing the good name of the *Neptune*? We had already named it the *Nightmare Ship Neptune*.

'You know she was the only one there not of good name,' Lucky Gem spat, pointing at me. 'The only one not a lady or gentleman.'

'Not the only one,' D'Arcy said firmly, staring down Lucky Gem, who held the stare. But while D'Arcy's stare was firm yet relaxed, Gem's looked like he was ready to attack.

'Lucky Gem is right,' Captain Trail said. 'And I warned you, Wentworth. You took the girl ashore, you were responsible for her actions.'

'I didn't take anything!' I shouted, unable to hold it in any longer. 'I looked at the candlestick, but I didn't take anything. It was Lucky Gem. I know it was. He was there too.'

'Molly!' D'Arcy said sharply, but it was too late. I had spoken, and I paid the price, as Captain Trail stepped forward and his hand struck the side of my face. I cried out, tears blurring my vision, pain stinging my cheek.

'Your words have betrayed your guilt, girl,' Captain Trail said, stepping back. 'I didn't once name the item. You would do well to keep your mouth closed.'

'And you would do well never to lay a hand on her again,' D'Arcy said, stepping forward.

'You overstep yourself, Wentworth,' Trail responded.

146

'And you,' D'Arcy said, 'should watch your hand, lest mine fly towards you.'

I marvelled then, as I was to in the future, at how D'Arcy remained so calm. While everyone around him seemed to lose their temper, he stayed as cool as the air off the ocean.

'Besides,' D'Arcy said, 'I can promise you, the girl took nothing.'

'Is that right?' sneered the Captain. 'And how can you promise that?'

'Because Molly was correct,' D'Arcy said, his expression never changing. 'It was a candlestick, and I took it.'

'NO!' I cried, my exclamation matched by a sharp laugh from Lucky Gem.

'I knew it,' he said. 'I knew it were one of 'em. Probably set it up together, they did, planned it all along.'

'Quiet, Gem,' Captain Trail said, setting his gaze on D'Arcy with a look I had never seen before, a look that sent chills through my entire body. 'I'm not surprised,' he continued. 'I knew of your past before we set sail, Wentworth. I knew already of your thievery. Where is it? Where is the candlestick?'

I stared at D'Arcy. Thievery? But he was on the ship as a passenger, a paying passenger. Had he paid with ill-gotten funds? Had he taken a place on-board while my father, an innocent man, was left to die with the convicts?

'It is in a safe place,' D'Arcy said. 'I shall return it to you when we land, so you can send it back to the Governor, as promised.'

'You will give it to me now!' roared Captain Trail. 'You will give it to me when I say so! I run this ship, not you! You will cause no more embarrassment!'

'It is of no use to you now,' D'Arcy said, again, amazingly calm.

'Then you shall rot,' Captain Trail said. 'Until you supply the candlestick, you shall rot in chains!'

And with that, D'Arcy was taken away. He offered no resistance, but as he left he turned to look at me. It was a look that told me of his innocence, and if so, he had saved me, again. And yet a feeling rolled in the pit of my stomach, put there by Captain Trail's words, a feeling that told me perhaps D'Arcy had taken the candlestick, that perhaps he was a criminal after all.

A criminal I had trusted. A criminal who, perhaps, had used me as a cover to commit another crime.

CHAPTER 16: THE ARGUMENT

D'Arcy was locked and chained in his quarters. As a paying passenger, and one who was only suspected of a crime but not yet found guilty, despite his admission, Captain Trail was unable to put him with the other men in the hold of the ship.

Much to the Captain's disappointment.

'You will be treated as one of them,' he sneered to D'Arcy's face. 'You shall be fed what they're fed and chained as they're chained. And this only till the candlestick is given over, then you will be thrown in with the rest of the thievin' rats. And, along with that, just in case you're guilty … 40 lashes. Tomorrow.'

I longed to go to D'Arcy, to ask him of all this, of why he had spoken, of what he had done.

And of his innocence, which I was convinced of, and yet … no, not D'Arcy Wentworth. Not the charming, heroic, gentle D'Arcy Wentworth.

But why had Captain Trail mentioned thievery? Was it more lies, more attempts to set D'Arcy up, to frame him as my father had been framed?

It was all so confusing, and Tattie was no help. She wouldn't stop talking about it, while I was trying to get my head around things, trying to sort out the jumble of thoughts.

'Maybe 'e did somethin' back in the old country,' she was saying. 'Maybe stole somethin' to give to a lady. Maybe he stole an 'orse to escape after robbin' a gentleman. Maybe it was murder! Oh my, Molly, 'ave we been consortin' with a murderer all this time? I can't believe it, this is so excitin'!'

Of our entire time on board the *Neptune*, Tattie had been a source of comfort to me. She had cheered me up, made me smile, and helped me more than anyone through the passing of my parents.

But right now, her voice was like nails on glass. I felt the heat rising in me, trying to think, unable to concentrate, needing silence, wanting isolation.

And then it exploded out of me,

'Be quiet, Tattie!' I yelled, making not only Tattie stop speaking but all the women. 'For once in your life, be quiet!'

Tattie's mouth hung open, her eyes starting to glisten.

'Please,' I continued, my voice quieter now but no less firm. 'I need to be able to think about this, but it is too hard while you talk.'

'But talkin's the only way we're goin' to sort this 'ere mess out, Princess,' Tattie said. 'Anyway, as I was sayin' -'

'No, Tattie,' I interrupted. 'Not this time. And you need to stop calling me Princess. From now on. Just stop, please, stop your natter.'

'Oh, well, sorry, madam,' Tattie said. 'What, is this now you've been accused of stealin'? Per'aps you *did* take that candlestick. Per'aps D'Arcy Wentworth took the fall for you, and 'ere you are all snug in our quarters with a candlestick 'idden somewhere, while 'e sits in chains.'

'I didn't steal it, Tattie!' I said, standing. She stood as well, facing me.

'Is that right?' she said, nose to nose with me. 'You're so 'igh 'n' mighty you could never be so low as to steal somethin', I s'pose.'

'That's right,' I said. 'After all, of the two of us, there's only one capable of doing such a thing, and I'm no thieving convict!'

Tattie gasped, as did the other women. I stared around in shock.

'I'm sorry,' I said, my hand slapping over my mouth, my voice a whisper. 'I'm sorry I said that.'

Tattie whirled around and walked off on me.

'Tattie, please, wait, I'm sorry, I didn't -'

'Leave 'er be, Molly,' Catherine said, her voice soft and kind, as usual, but there was an edge to it I had not heard before. 'And perhaps take some time for yourself too. Think about what you just said, and what the women in 'ere 'ave done for you.'

I nodded, trying to control my emotions, but it was too much. I cried, softly at first, then in a flood. Everything I had held in couldn't be held any longer.

And from the women, these brave, wonderful women who had helped me say goodbye to both my parents, I got nothing. Not a word of sympathy. Not a consoling arm around my shoulder.

Nothing.

'Sir, may the girl walk on deck?' I heard Catherine say. 'She ain't feeling well.'

'What do I care?' was the reply. It was the feeling I was getting in the room as well.

Catherine came back to me.

'Go on, girl,' she said. 'Come on back in when you're ready to say your apology.'

She gently ushered me outside, the cool wind hitting me square in the face, ice on my tears. I turned back to speak to Catherine, to anyone, but they were gone.

I was on the deck, and I was all alone.

***

I stood at the ship's railing for a time, staring into nothingness, my thoughts swirling and crashing like the waves. The air had become cooler since we had left Cape Town, and from what D'Arcy had told me while we were there, it would get cooler still.

'We left in winter, Molly, travelled through to the start of spring, and now we shall follow winter around the globe as we near our new home.'

I couldn't get my head around that, that we were basically in winter all year round. That the world had different seasons, that we were not all one and the same.

I felt ill at that thought, of us being one and the same. I had used the differences between Tattie and me, our differing reasons for being on the *Neptune*, as a way to stop her talking, to try and think. It had come out wrong, but I was at the edge of the cliff and felt like she was trying to push me over it.

I felt lost and alone and scared and cold and tired, and I just wanted my mam to hold me and my da to bring me a warm drink and tell me a story. They had always made everything alright, and now they weren't here, I didn't know if anything would ever be alright again.

I wandered the deck for a long time. No one paid me any heed. It was as though, now they had D'Arcy locked away, I posed no threat to them.

Two men stood guard at the door to his quarters, though from what I had seen of the chains the convicts were in, there would be little to no chance of D'Arcy escaping anyway.

I passed the guards, who ignored me, which was just as well, for then I was able to slip to the back of the quarters, where I found a small porthole.

And no guards.

It was time to put some of what Tattie had taught me into practice.

I tapped on the porthole, aiming to be loud enough for D'Arcy to hear, but not anyone else.

There was no response.

I tried again, a little harder, and heard a stirring from within.

'Yes?' came the quiet reply. I prayed those at the door wouldn't hear it.

'It's me,' I said, standing on the tips of my toes, getting as close to the opening as possible. 'Molly. You know, the girl.'

I shook my head in dismay. I was talking nonsense!

'I believe I recall you, yes,' D'Arcy said, with humour lacing his words.

'Why?' was all I said. It was all he needed.

'Tell me, Molly O'Hanlon. If Tattie was in trouble, or your family, what would you do to help them?'

I thought of my parents, of Tattie, of D'Arcy himself, and I stood tall.

'Anything, Mr Wentworth. Anything at all.'

'And there is your answer, Molly,' he replied. 'You are as family to me, and so I did anything at all.'

'But they shall flog you,' I said, and it took a mighty effort to keep my voice low.

'Yes, Molly, which is a thousand times better than if they had flogged you.'

I choked back a tear and asked that which I dreaded.

'Mr Wentworth,' I said, 'I believe with all my heart I know the answer, but I must hear you say the words. Captain Trail said you have committed crimes before. Is it true? Tell me it isn't. Tell me you didn't take the candlestick. Please tell me you didn't. I don't know how I shall cope if you did.'

There was silence. It felt as though my heart stopped beating as I waited forever for the answer.

'Molly,' D'Arcy said, 'before I say this, I need you to swear you will not repeat it to anyone, even Tattie. You can say you presume it to be true, but you must not say I uttered the words. Do you swear?'

I nodded, lost for words, then realised that was not helpful, so I said I promised.

'Molly,' D'Arcy said. 'What Captain Trail said about me was indeed true. Do you recall what I said when Lucky Gem hit his head? That he wouldn't testify against you?'

I replied that I did.

'I knew that because I myself have been before a Magistrate, rightfully accused more than once of taking money from those who believed themselves above me, who had refused to pay me money I had fully earned.'

'How did you earn it?' I asked.

'That,' D'Arcy said, 'is a tale for another time. Let me just say it was an establishment these people did not want to admit they frequented. An establishment where games were played for money. And so, to testify against me meant to testify of their attendance. So yes, I stole, Molly, but

I believe I stole in a right cause, if there is such a thing. However, I promise with all that I am that I did not take that candlestick.'

My heart finally released itself from my throat as I breathed out in a rush, then just as quickly ducked into a small gap as some men walked past. When they were gone, I resurfaced.

'Mr Wentworth, I promise you this. I will find the person who took the candlestick and set you up. This cannot happen again. It just can't.'

'I understand, Molly, I truly do, but you must not put yourself in danger. I know I can't stop you, so please, be sure to have Tattie help you in anything you do. She's a good girl, that one, and she knows ways to stay safe in dangerous situations.'

I sighed.

'I don't know if Tattie will help me,' I said. 'I was horrible to her. She may never forgive me again.'

There was a silence, again, and when he spoke, D'Arcy changed my world.

'Molly, even among the best of friends there will always be rough seas. But all rough seas eventually smooth. Sometimes the storm lasts for days, sometimes longer, but we have one advantage over the ocean.'

'What's that?' I asked, trying my hardest to follow.

'We get to decide when the winds die down, and when the thunder stops. Do you understand what I'm saying?'

I replied that I did, and I thought that was the truth, though I also realised I didn't know the full truth of it.

But I knew enough.

'I shall talk to Tattie now,' I said. 'And the other women too. I'm scared, Mr Wentworth. I'm scared they hate me.'

'Feeling scared is natural, Molly,' he said. 'We all feel scared. It is in feeling scared and still acting that heroines are born. Go on now, before you are seen with a thieving criminal.'

He chuckled, and though I tried a couple more times to converse with him, he wouldn't answer. I knew that was his way of saying it was time.

Time for me to face the music.

CHAPTER 17: THE APOLOGY

I returned to our quarters and stood in front of all the women. I had asked them to hear me out, and although some of them hadn't wanted to listen (and when I say some of them I mean Tattie) Catherine had helped me to gain their attention.

Catherine really was lovely, and really seemed to be looking out for me, just like D'Arcy had asked her to.

But gathering them was the easy part. Now, standing in front of them, all eyes on me (except for Tattie. She refused to look and sat facing the wall), I felt small and frightened.

No, not frightened, terrified.

How could I do this? How could I speak to them, apologise for what I said? I had no excuse. I had been through so much, but so had each and every one of them.

I held onto my mother's locket and squeezed it, then closed my eyes. I imagined D'Arcy, how calm he always was, no matter the situation.

I imagined my mother, smiling at me, saying she was proud of me.

But it still wasn't enough.

And then, then I imagined my father, telling a story, his eyes alive. I imagined him looking at me on that last day, saying I was always with him, and I knew, right then, standing in front of those women, not knowing what to say, that my father was always with me too.

I opened my eyes, I looked at each and every one of them, I ignored my trembling hands, and I spoke.

'I'm sorry,' I said, looking down, unable to keep eye contact any longer. 'What I said was … it was so …'

I was struggling. I took a deep breath in, then let it out, and tried again.

'My father was a wonderful man,' I said. '*Is* a wonderful man. Though he shan't speak to me again, not for real, I hear his voice every single day. But he's dead, my da, killed by this ship and the people who sail it. He shouldn't have been here. I shouldn't have been here. That's what makes me so mad. That's what made me so mad the other day, to think I was accused too. That I could end up … like my da. Or Mr Wentworth. Now he's in trouble for something he didn't do as well, and tomorrow he'll be lashed and it's all my fault.'

Silence greeted my words, but all their eyes, save Tattie's were fixed on me.

'My ma too. Everyone's gone. Why am *I* still here?

160

Why?'

I yelled the last word, staring at them, crying.

I was still greeted with silence. I tried to keep my voice level, like D'Arcy always did, but I was too far gone now, and the words came out in a jumble of tears and yelling.

'I don't want to be here, and I hate it, but at the same time if I wasn't here I would never have met Mr Wentworth. Or Margaret. Or Catherine. Or any of you brave women. Or my best friend in the whole world who I made mad and who hates me now and all I want to do is give her a hug and have her make me laugh and I can't because she hates me and I already said that but it's true.'

My chest was heaving when I finished, my face wet with tears. No one said a word, but now all eyes turned to Tattie. She kept facing the wall.

'I lost everyone,' I said. 'I can't lose you too, Tattie.'

She breathed deep but stayed watching the wall.

'Tattie?' I asked softly. Her shoulder twitched, but she didn't turn.

'Tattie?' I asked again, a little louder. 'Please?'

I sensed her wanting to turn but she resisted.

'TATTIE!' yelled Margaret.

Still she didn't turn, and my anger burst out of me.

'AGH!' I groaned. 'You are the most stubborn, silly, frustrating, stinky ... ummm ... ummmm ...'

I was lost for words, and then, ever so quietly, a word came from my best friend.

'Funny?' she said, before turning around, a grin on that cheeky face of hers.

'Incredible? Best ever? Amazing?' she asked, getting up now, and walking towards me, a step with every word. The women started smiling, some of them with tears in their eyes. Tattie kept going.

'Clever? Pretty? Wonderful? Lovely?'

I watched her, tears streaming down my face now.

'Annoying,' I said, making her laugh. 'Evil for making me wait.'

'Well, what are you waitin' for then?' she asked, spreading her arms wide. 'Come and give yer best friend a hug!'

I ran to her, covering the distance in an instant, holding her tight, unable to stop crying.

'I …can't … lose … you … too … Tattie,' I sobbed. She held me tighter, and now the other women joined in the hug, all of us holding each other.

'You ain't never going to, Princess,' Tattie said, and although I had said, in anger, I didn't want her to call me that anymore, in that moment it was perfect.

Because it was Tattie.

'None of us will leave you, Molly,' Margaret said, stroking the back of my head. 'Not while we have breath in our bodies, we won't. All of us here, we're a family. An oddball family, no doubt, but a family just the same.'

'Now,' Tattie said. 'How are we going to get that Mr Wentworth free then? I'm guessin' you 'ave some sort of plan cookin', Molly O'Hanlon?'

I pulled away from her and smiled through the tears.

'I'm going to need your help though,' I said before looking at the others. 'All of you,' I continued. 'If you'll help me, I will be forever grateful.'

'Oh, Molly,' Catherine said, shocking some of the other women who were yet to hear her speak much at all, 'we wouldn't have it any other way. Right, everyone?'

'RIGHT!' everyone yelled.

'Right,' said Tattie. 'Now then, you tell us what you need us to do.'

I grinned again, despite feeling fear course through me. It was time for heroines to be born.

CHAPTER 18: THE CRIME

The plan was simple, but one I hoped against hope would work. It would put everything I had learned to the test but, if it worked, it would free D'Arcy and, hopefully, clear my father's name.

We would need to be clever, quiet, and we would also need our fair share of good luck.

The first bit of luck came the following morning. Adeline, heavy with child, started howling in pain.

And this time, she wasn't pretending.

'The baby's coming,' Margaret said, rushing to Adeline's side. 'Tattie, get Dr Gray now.'

'Oh, 'e won't believe me,' Tattie said. 'Not after last time.'

'Tattie's right,' I said. 'I'll go.'

'No, Molly,' Catherine said. 'Not only is it dangerous, but you have other roles to play today.'

She was right, and I was glad she was finding her voice more each day. I liked Catherine and hoped we would share many times together in the new land. In the meantime, my part in the plan was to stall the flogging of D'Arcy, while Tattie shadowed Lucky Gem, to tease out his guilt.

'What would D'Arcy do,' I whispered to myself. 'Come on, Molly O'Hanlon, make him proud. Show him you have learned well.'

I sat with my head in my hands and then it came to me. Of course! It was obvious! I turned to Tattie.

'I was thinking of what Mr Wentworth would do,' I said. 'I was trying to remember what I had learned from him, and I shall use all of that, but Tattie, most importantly, I shall use what I have learned from you.'

'I 'ave no idea what you're talkin' about, Princess,' she said, staring at me blankly. Catherine, however, realised immediately.

'Are you sure, Molly?' she asked. 'I don't know if ...'

'Mr Wentworth would trust me, Catherine,' I said. 'I swear to you, I will be careful.'

She nodded.

'You're a brave girl, just like he said.'

I blushed, then two noises filled the air. The first was a wail from Adeline, then a shout from Tattie.

'Will someone tell me what's goin' on?' she screamed, breaking the tension and making us all laugh.

It also made me shoot into action.

'Tattie,' I said, 'I shall shadow Lucky Gem. You shall stall the flogging with a distraction, and Catherine, if it is alright with her, shall get Dr Gray. This shall also delay the flogging, as Dr Gray must be there when it occurs, seeing as his assistant, Mr Wentworth, is the one receiving the whip.'

Catherine visibly shuddered at that thought but nodded.

'If it shall help Mr Wentworth,' she said. 'I shall do it, despite my fears.'

Some of the other ladies giggled, though at the time I knew not why. Tattie looked at me.

'You reckon you're ready then?' she asked.

I nodded.

'I have had the best teacher possible,' I smiled. She hugged me.

'You be careful, Princess,' she said. 'We got a lot of friendship left to go yet.'

I nodded into her shoulder, then we had our second lot of luck, only this time it was of the bad sort.

A crack of thunder rumbled, and it sounded close.

There was a storm on its way.

***

Tattie hugged me again as we left our quarters.

'You can do this' she said. 'I ain't never seen no one learn to be sneaky quite so fast.'

I wasn't sure if that was a compliment or a tease, but she was gone before I could respond. I shook my head and smiled, and the mission was underway.

Despite the hour of the day, the skies were dark, and the thunder rumbled louder and closer as I snuck around the ship. While I had thought it to be bad luck, the weather actually provided extra cover, and when the rain began, I heard grumbles of men as they passed by.

I reached the area of the deck where the floggings took place. A crowd had gathered, despite the threat of a storm. D'Arcy was bound, hands above his head, his back bare. An image of my mother's wounds flashed through my mind and I flinched, especially when I saw the whip that was to be used.

'It's called a cat o' nine tails,' Tattie had told me one day. 'And it's a cruel weapon, Molly O'Hanlon.'

It certainly looked cruel. We needed to move, and fast.

But Captain Trail moved faster.

'Get it over and done with quickly,' he said. 'We must away before the storm.'

'No,' cried Catherine, running into view. I knew it would be terrifying to do such a thing, and marvelled at her courage to help Adeline, as well as D'Arcy. 'Dr Gray must come quickly. It's Adeline. The baby is coming.'

Dr Gray looked around, as if to determine whether he was being fooled again, but he knew Catherine, and he knew she was as honest as a convict could be.

He turned to Captain Trail.

'I must go,' he said. 'Though it is a convict, my oath as a doctor will not let her suffer.'

Captain Trail nodded.

'Be quick about it,' he said. 'The seas begin to swell. If the storm hits while we are stationery, we shall all suffer.'

Dr Gray nodded and rushed off with Adeline. I spotted Lucky Gem, standing at the front of the crowd, smiling gleefully as he looked at D'Arcy's bare back. Gem wanted blood, and he was about to get it.

I spotted Tattie in the crowd too, though no one else did. One of the other things she had taught me, aside from being able to hide, was the trick of seeing what others overlook.

'See what others don't even look for,' she had said. 'It ain't that people are blind, it's just they don't look.'

She waved to me and pulled a face at the man nearest her, almost making me laugh. I silently cursed her, then focused again. Then everything went wrong.

Captain Trail waited till Dr Gray was out of earshot, then he turned to the crowd.

'This man has stolen from the Governor of Cape Town. He has openly defied me throughout the journey and has cavorted with convicts.'

The crowd booed. A crack of thunder made me jump. What was Trail up to? I found out soon enough.

'Does he deserve a doctor to oversee the flogging?'

'No!' cried the crowd, the rain drowning out the sound before it left the area. 'No!'

'Should we wait, when all it shall do is put us, the good folk, in danger of the comin' storm?' the Captain asked, staring at the crowd.

'No!' they cried again, lightning flashing, lighting up Captain Trail's face. A face that held both a sneer of contempt as well as a smile of revenge.

'Then let the flogging begin,' he said, with a nod.

Suddenly, before Tattie or I could move, the whip was raised and came down with a mighty **CRACK!** I held in my scream, but only just, as I saw blood appear in a line on D'Arcy's back.

'No!' cried Tattie, risking all as she jumped out of the crowd. 'The candlestick has not been found. You can't do this, you can't!'

'Begone, you silly little girl,' Captain Trail said. 'I care not that the item has not been found. The prisoner has admitted his crime. I say he is guilty, and the discovery of the candlestick shall only confirm it. Then ...'

He paused. I could barely hear him now, over the rain, but his next words cut through me.

'Then, when we land and Wentworth hands over the candlestick, he shall be condemned to death. Now whip the accused.'

He nodded to the man with the whip, and then he also gave a small nod to Lucky Gem.

See what others don't even look for.

Lucky Gem slipped away and I followed, unseen. I prayed Tattie would play her part well as I left. I knew she would.

If not, this may all be for naught.

CRACK!

No! It had begun again, but the crack was followed by a scream, that of a girl and a gasp from the crowd. Oh Tattie, I thought, what have you done?

I didn't have any time to consider it further. Lucky Gem, his jacket pulled over his head, was moving quickly, and I was struggling to keep up.

I had to find out what he was up to, and why he had left the scene of the flogging.

***

I was like a ghost, staying close to Lucky Gem without him having a clue I was there. I saw him struggle with the lock to a small cabin. I heard him swear as he dropped the keys, forcing me to back away as they bounced along the deck towards me.

'Oi, what you doin', Gem?' a voice cried as he picked up the keys. I spun around. It was Henry, one of my father's tormentors. One of the men who had made my da's last days unbearable.

'Greetin's to ya, 'Enry,' Gem said. 'This 'ere is the final twist. Right now. Captain Trail, 'e's got this all sorted 'e 'as. We're makin' that girl get what she right deserves for thievin'.'

"Ang on now,' Henry said. 'It's Wentworth, 'e stole it right? 'E's tastin' the whip right now.'

Gem picked up the keys and grinned, a flash of lightning making him look even more evil.

'That's what you think, 'Enry, but 'ere's the thing,' he said, moving closer to Henry and therefore closer to me. I shrunk into the shadows, able to hear every word.

'We 'ad this all planned. See, Wentworth'll feel the sting of the cat o'nine tails alright, and 'e'll get extra too. Then I come out, after it's done, and I say, "Ho, there, Captain, I found the stick, but it were the girl 'ad 'idden it!" Then the girl'll get a taste of the whip too. You remember what she did at the start, with you and 'er dad. She's been sneakin' round deck, thinks she owns the ship, she does. Well, not for much longer she won't. And I need 'er gone, I do. She'll be the second O'Hanlon I done set up, and she'll be the last.'

It took everything I had not to rush out. To scream. To scratch, claw, bite. To gain revenge. To satisfy my aching soul.

But I didn't. I froze. Henry hadn't answered but Lucky Gem laughed and opened the cabin, emerging not long after with the candlestick in hand.

And then I did move. Hiding was no longer a concern. I needed that candlestick, and I needed it now, to save D'Arcy, to save myself, and to get Lucky Gem to confess his framing of my da.

He was responsible for my father's death. The man was a murderer, though he had not struck the final blow himself.

I flew from my hiding spot, knocking the candlestick from Lucky Gem's hands. He cried out in shock, but when I turned to retrieve it, the slippery deck foiled me and I skidded into the side of the ship, knocking the air out of me. A shock of pain roared through my side like fire.

'I heard you,' I said, gasping for breath. 'I know it was you, and now there's a witness. You will tell of how you framed my father!'

Lucky Gem laughed out loud, moving towards the candlestick.

'Girl, you don't know a thing. 'Enry 'ere don't mind none of what I did, and 'alf the ship knows I took a turn for me freedom. They don't care none about your da seein' his last days, filthy criminal or not.'

'I CARE!' I screamed, on my feet in an instant, diving for the object that would free D'Arcy. But Henry and Lucky Gem also dove for it and we crashed together. Being by far the lightest, I was sent spinning along the deck.

The ship lurched on a wave, and the candlestick rolled clear of us.

'Get 'er,' growled Lucky Gem. 'We'll take 'er with us.'

Henry lunged for me, but I easily eluded him, tripping him up as I went. He fell with a cry but reached out and grabbed my leg, making me fall as well. My head hit the deck, stunning me, and that was enough for Lucky Gem to grab me and lift me to my feet.

Once again, his foul breath filled my nostrils, and I gagged, his hand tight around my throat.

'You ain't been nothin' but trouble, girl,' he said. 'You done near ruined everythin', you did. But it's over now, you 'ear me?'

He shook me as he stared into my eyes, making him laugh.

'Yeah, that's right. Only thing is, while you're still 'ere, you can deny it. So maybe we're all better off without you 'ere at all.'

'Hang on there, Gem,' Henry said. 'This don't seem right.'

'Quiet, 'Enry,' Gem said. 'You be quiet and you get out if you ain't got the stomach for it.'

There was a mighty crack, and I didn't know if it was the whip striking D'Arcy yet again or thunder. I didn't have time to think on it either, for Lucky Gem carried me to the ship's railing and held me over the edge.

'So long, girlie,' he said. 'And this time, you ain't able to bite.'

He pushed me a little further, one hand on my throat, the other holding the front of my tunic. The rain pelted into my face, my eyes, merging with my tears.

I'm sorry, Da, I thought. D'Arcy. Mam. I'm sorry I couldn't make it right.

Then I closed my eyes and I waited for the end.

CHAPTER 19: THE STORM

Suddenly, the boat jolted as the anchor was lifted, and we were away. I knew this meant the flogging of D'Arcy had ended.

It also meant Lucky Gem lost his grip on my throat and I slipped over the ship's railing, screaming. Panic caused him to grip onto my tunic harder, stopping me from falling, even though that had been his intention.

'Gem, **NO!'** Henry yelled. 'Not a girl, Gem. That's too far.'

Lucky Gem pulled me up, and for a split second I believed, I truly believed, he was going to haul me back onto deck, that he was going to let me live.

But he just sneered at me again, steadying himself as the ship careened left and right on the rising waves.

'This ain't just a girl' he said. 'She's caused more trouble than she's worth. But she won't cause no more.'

He lifted me so I sat on the edge of the ship's railing. I sat there, frozen, waiting, wanting to kick out at him, but knowing if I did that I would surely fall.

'No!' cried Henry.

I looked directly into Lucky Gem's eyes and said as calmly as D'Arcy had taught me to, 'You shall sleep every night with blood on your hands. Mine. My father's. My mother's. You shall spend eternity thinking about the pain you have caused.'

He grinned.

'Fine with me,' he said, and his hand loosened its grip on my tunic.

And then, out of nowhere, something or someone thudded into Lucky Gem, knocking him to the deck. In doing so he let go of me and I screamed, waving my arms, losing my balance, before strong hands grabbed me and pulled me onto the ship.

It was then I saw what had saved me, what had knocked him down. I had assumed it was Henry, but he stood staring.

It had been the women.

It had been my family.

Every single woman from our quarters, save Adeline, was there. It was them who had knocked Gem down. And it had been three of them who had hauled me to safety. They closed in around Gem.

'Get the Captain, 'Enry,' he said, sneering. There was a flash of lightning and I saw something in his hand. The candlestick! He had it once again!

'No, Gem,' Henry said. 'I done things on this ship I ain't proud of, but that there girl, these 'ere women, they done showed me a better path to take.'

''Enry!' screamed Lucky Gem, pointing the candlestick at him. 'Do you know who I am? I'm the Captain's man, I am. Now go get 'im so these women can be flogged, and you alongside 'em.'

'Not today, you foul beast,' said Margaret, stepping forward. 'Today, you get a floggin' of your own.'

The grin faded as Lucky Gem saw the look on the women's faces, and he knew he was outnumbered. He took a step back and then suddenly the bolt of lightning was back, as out of the rain and darkness flew Tattie, teeth bared, crashing into Gem, scratching at him, screaming at him.

'You tried to kill my best friend!' she screamed.

Gem threw her off him, sending her sliding along the deck.

'Tattie!' I screamed.

'He's runnin',' cried one of the women, and he was. Gem had taken off, sprinting, taking the candlestick with him.

Teeth bared, Tattie crashes into Lucky Gem

'No!' I screamed, launching myself after him, only to be knocked from my feet as another wave struck the boat. Although I could hear cries from the crew as they worked to keep the ship upright, I could hear also Lucky Gem's cackles of glee as he ran, the women in pursuit.

Another wave sent me rolling forward, crashing into Tattie.

'He has the candlestick, Tattie,' I said. 'We must stop him!'

We lurched again, rolling along the deck, and suddenly I saw Lucky Gem running towards us! The women were close behind and were cornering him.

Tattie and I leapt to our feet and charged at Lucky Gem, then a wave crashed over the edge of the ship! I was tossed around, crashed around. I somehow got to my feet, pain scorching through my side. I focused and saw Lucky Gem standing facing the women, facing Tattie, facing me.

'I couldn't throw you overboard,' he said, jabbing the candlestick in my direction, 'but this is just as good. Without your precious candlestick, you ain't never provin' no one innocent.'

Suddenly, his face changed to one of shock. So did mine, and I ducked down. But it was too late for Lucky Gem.

We had both seen the wave looming above him.

The wave that crashed over the edge of the ship.

The wave that swept Lucky Gem overboard.

The wave that punished him for the murder of my mother and father.

He was gone ... but with him was the candlestick. My parents were avenged, but D'Arcy was still a prisoner.

***

Tattie helped me to my feet and we moved as well as we could to shelter, the ship still riding the waves, my side still on fire, burning. There was no blood, and I had no clue as to what had happened.

'It's your ribs, Princess,' Tattie said. 'I'll bet more'n me life they're well broken, they are.'

I sighed, which only sent more pain rushing through me. I flinched again as I saw Henry standing in front of me.

'It's okay, girl,' he said. 'I spoke the truth before. What Gem done, what 'e tried to do, that weren't okay, that weren't. I'll come with you. I'll tell the Captain what I know, no matter the cost.'

I nodded my thanks.

'Get 'er to her bunk,' Henry said. 'Let 'er rest.'

'Mr Wentworth,' I said. 'Where is he?'

I suddenly remembered something from earlier.

'Tattie!' I gasped. 'You were struck by the whip?'

Tattie grinned at me.

'I got me a battle wound, I did,' she said. I couldn't believe she had been whipped and could still laugh. Then, when Henry and the other women had gone, Tattie leaned in and whispered in my ear.

'Oi, Molly, it 'urt like 'eck, it did! Still burns like fire right now. But I'd do it again, I would. Any day of the week if it 'elped you, or that nice Mr Wentworth.'

I didn't remember much more of that night, only being led to my bunk, laid on it, and then each woman coming and giving me a hug and a kiss on the forehead, each woman playing the part of my mother, my sister, my aunt, my everything.

I had a family.

I was safe.

CHAPTER 20: THE BIRTHDAY

Weeks later, as I sat on the deck just outside the women's quarters, gazing into the distance, the horrific events of the voyage seemed like a nightmare. Not real, yet still terrifying.

But when I saw Tattie's scar from the cat o' nine tails, or I held Adeline's baby, or felt a twinge in my side, or lay down every single night and remembered my mother, I knew how real it had all been, and how I missed my parents so.

I sighed and crossed my legs, taking out a piece of paper and some charcoal, and I began to write some of my memories. As much as I wanted to avoid writing about the hard parts of the voyage, I knew I would be unable to avoid them.

'You're a very studious young lady,' a voice said, a presence by my side. 'It will hold you in good stead in the future.'

I nodded but didn't look up, as I was working on a word I wasn't sure how to spell.

'Close,' said D'Arcy Wentworth, sitting by my side. 'But you have left out an e.'

I put the e in.

'No,' he said. 'Not at the start. It goes at the end.'

I blushed and scribbled out the whole word, making him laugh.

'You'll get there, Molly. In fact, I do believe you will get anywhere you wish.'

I looked at him now. I wasn't sure why it was hard sometimes. Perhaps it was the memory of my parents. Perhaps it was the knowledge that he had a criminal past, or perhaps it was just the fact I was so grateful he was free once more, yet I felt so guilty for the scars I knew would cover his skin after his flogging.

The one Tattie had tried to stop.

The one that had happened because of me.

'You know, Molly,' D'Arcy said, looking out over the edge of the boat, 'when we arrive at the new land, it shall mean new beginnings. For all of us. We have all lost, either on this voyage or before.'

'Not you,' I said. 'You have everything.'

He shook his head.

'If only that were so.' His voice had gone soft, his eyes staring out over the water but seeing something long gone. 'You see, Molly, I am a paying passenger, as you know.'

I nodded.

'Have you ever wondered why I would leave my life in London to go to a land where anything could happen? Where a new colony is beginning? On a voyage that could well have ended me?'

'Could have ended you because of me,' I said.

'No, Molly, because this ship has held horrors none of us expected, though perhaps I should have. Still, none of that matters. What I have left behind is something that was mine, yet could never be mine.'

'I don't understand,' I said. 'If you had it, how could it not be yours?'

'It's like Stig, it is,' said Tattie, walking up. I had no idea what she was talking about, and then suddenly I burst out laughing.

'Stig!' I cried. 'You never told me of Stig! Your long, lost love! The hairy man with the wet nose!'

Tattie laughed as well.

'Princess, he was a wonder, but he weren't no man. He was a dog, he was, the cutest mongrel I ever did see! And he loved me more than life itself. Ain't that the same thing, Mr Wentworth?'

D'Arcy looked at Tattie curiously.

'Yes,' he said warily. 'How did you know?'

Tattie shrugged.

'Sometimes I just knows, I does,' was all she said. D'Arcy nodded. I was confused out of my mind.

'I don't understand. Did you have a dog too, Mr Wentworth?'

Tattie and D'Arcy burst into laughter, leaving me to wonder what was funny, and what was going on at all.

Sometimes, to be eleven is to feel like a baby.

***

Not long after, as I lay on my bunk, the women's area was quiet. That was not a common occurrence, what with a new baby, a group of women who had become firm friends after near on six months at sea and, of course, Tattie, who was rarely if ever quiet.

I breathed in the last remnants of my mother. Suddenly, I sensed a presence behind me. I rolled over and gasped. All the woman stood there, looking at me. D'Arcy was there too, and even Henry, had shown himself to be a man of honour and bravery, and had become a friend to us all.

'What is it?' I asked. 'Is the baby unwell?'

They smiled, and then Tattie sat on my bunk.

'It might be after it 'ears this,' she said. 'But we've been practising real 'ard, we have, Molly. Real 'ard. This is for you, from all of us.'

And then the entire group of women, along with D'Arcy and Henry, began to sing, and it took only one word before I began to sob.

For this is what they sang.

'There was a girl called Molly, she was so very small,
But every time we looked at her, well we felt eight foot tall.
When she was a baby, she screamed and screamed so loud,
She does that sometimes still but Molly, you make us so proud.

You're brave and you are clever, you're generous as well,
With every day that passes, Molly, you make our hearts swell.
Our love for you is endless, our love for you is true,
Molly, you're our darling and we'll always be with you.

You're a gift to us, my dear, in every single way,
*So happy birthday, Molly, hooray, hooray, **HOORAY!***'

They finished and burst into applause, and I did as well, though I could barely see anything now through the tears.

'She taught us, Molly,' D'Arcy said, when the noise died down. 'She knew she may not make it, and so she taught us.'

I nodded, trying to wipe my face at the same time, but it was all too much. It was wonderful and terrible and incredible and sad all at once, and before I knew it, I was being held by the women, by my new family, and they were crying with me, both for my losses and their own, and we mourned together and I thanked them over and over again, and I knew, right then, that I would never be alone.

***

'You know,' Tattie said. 'Now you're twelve, you need to get yourself a job.'

I laughed and pushed her.

'You are older than me,' I said, 'and have never had a job in your life.'

'Not true,' she said. 'I just don't 'ave a boss. I work for meself.'

'Yes,' I said. 'Pickpocketing.'

She shrugged.

'On occasion.'

I looked at her.

'Tattie, what is it? You're acting strangely.'

She returned my gaze.

'You remember the night Lucky Gem took a swim. A long swim. A very long swim.'

I nodded, unsure why she was returning to that night.

'Well, you also remember it were a real storm?'

I nodded again.

'And I was so brave leapin' on that dangerous villain?'

I nodded again, smiling but still confused beyond belief.

'I'd been unsure, I 'ad, about showin' you this,' Tattie said, reaching into her pocket. 'I kept it 'idden this whole time. But now I reckon you're a grown lady, you're ready to see it. I *am* a pickpocket, Molly, it 'elped me survive on the street. And now it 'elped me get this. 'Appy birthday, Princess.'

She opened her hand and in it she held a gem, a beautiful, orange, teardrop-shaped gem.

'What is it?' I breathed. 'And where did you get it.'

'This were on Lucky Gem,' she said. 'He 'ad it in 'is shirt pocket, 'e did. When I jumped on 'im, my 'and may 'ave slipped in and took it. I didn't know if it would be too sad for you but it feels right to give it to you.'

I took it. It was beautiful, for sure, but it also held such terrible memories.

'I don't know if I can keep it, Tattie,' I said. 'This belonged to the man who ...'

My voice trailed off and Tattie grinned at me.

'Oh, it ain't for keepin', Princess,' she said. 'Come on.'

She looked left and right, and then grabbed my hand and we ran along the deck, invisible to anyone who may catch us. Suddenly, Tattie stopped.

'This is it,' she said, then she turned to me. 'This is where that mongrel washed overboard. This is where you lost the chance for clearin' your da's name. This is where you get that chance now.'

She took my hand that held the gem.

'Finish it, Molly O'Hanlon,' she said. 'Throw that last bit of Lucky Gem as far as you can. Do it for your parents, Princess. Do it for them.'

'It must be worth a fortune, Tattie,' I said. 'How can I throw it away?'

'Because you hafta. Any money you received would stink. Like 'e did haha. Now throw, and when you do, yell loud as the storm we 'ad.'

'But we'll be caught,' I said, wide-eyed.

'Just let 'em try,' Tattie said, grinning. 'Now throw! And yell! Like this ... *AAAAGGGGHHHH!*'

I looked at my wild, carefree friend. She was wonderful, so very, very wonderful. I pulled back my arm, grinned at her, and then with a mighty heave threw that gem far, far away and as I did I roared.

'AAAGGGHHH!'

'Yeah, Molly!' Tattie cried. *'YEEEEAAAHHHHHHHH!'*

'Oi!' came a shout. 'What's goin' on?'

Tattie looked at me, eyes gleaming.

'Run!' she said, and we did. We ran and laughed and dodged and skidded and for the first time in a long time, I felt alive.

CHAPTER 21: THE LANDING

The next day I finished my chores in the women's quarters early. Tattie was still busy with hers, so I had some time to myself. I decided to go and see D'Arcy.

Although nothing had changed in terms of women and girls being able to walk the ship, D'Arcy had somehow convinced Captain Trail that I was allowed to, that I was to help him with various things, that he was training me in the ways of medicine.

All of this was true, of course, but that still didn't explain why Captain Trail said it would be okay. It was most unlike him.

'Do you remember what I said when we went inside the Castle of Good Hope?' D'Arcy asked. My mind went back, but all I could see was the glory, the amazing decorations, and, of course, my thoughts went to the slaves.

'You said to treat slaves well, but I don't see how that applies here.'

'It applies everywhere, Molly, and I have seen you treating all manner of people well on this trip … save perhaps, Lucky Gem, but that is another matter.'

I blushed and looked away. D'Arcy laid a hand on my shoulder.

'I said being able to converse with all manner of men is a worthy skill. As is knowing what they desire. That is what applies here.'

'What do you mean?' I asked, confused. D'Arcy shook his head.

'The details are not important, but certainly what has happened on this ship has given me leverage of sorts. Now, while my conversation with Captain Trail was important, it is not the most important detail I must tell you.'

I looked back at him now, just as a cry burst into the air.

'Land ho!'

We both stood, and suddenly Tattie was by my side as well.

'Land ho nothin'', she said, glaring over the waters. 'That's my call to make.' Then she turned and flashed her wicked grin, the grin that meant fun or trouble was afoot

'Maybe some people didn't 'ear 'him,' she said. She spun and ran off at top speed, yelling with all her might.

'Land! It's land, it is, and I saw it! *LAND!'*

'We know!' yelled a voice back. 'We already heard.'

That just made Tattie yell louder!

'Thank you for everything, Mr Wentworth,' I said. 'I don't know if I shall see you once we land. I don't know what I shall do at all.'

'Well now,' D'Arcy said, 'Tattie cut in before I was able to finish my sentence. I said when we were due to leave our homes that I would be here for you, I would look after you, and though this voyage has made me realise you are more than capable of looking after yourself, still it should not be so.'

I didn't know what he was going to say next, but I did know I was barely breathing.

'Molly, I have begun to teach you some of what I know, and I would like that to continue. If you accept, I should like you to stay with me. I shall also be employing Catherine and, if she so desires, and if we have space, Tattie is welcome to stay with us as well. Your training has only just begun, it seems a shame to finish it so early.'

I gasped and threw myself at him, feeling as impulsive as Tattie would have been. This was what I had wanted to hear. This meant I had a future. This meant I had a family.

***

I stood arm-in-arm with Tattie, D'Arcy beside us, as the ship slowly drew to a near stop, and then, as the anchor was dropped and we waved to people on-shore awaiting our arrival, I took a deep, deep breath. Our voyage to New South Wales had begun more than six months earlier and for many of those aboard it had been a perilous, miserable and fatal experience.

When we left Plymouth there were over 600 people aboard the ship. By the time we reached our new home, 161 of these, including my mam and da, had died. For those of us who had managed to survive the ordeal, it had been a test of our strength, courage and hopefulness. And it was this hopefulness that I was now clinging to as the shores of New South Wales came into view.

The anchor sunk into the waters below us, but my heart was flying. This marked the end of our journey aboard the nightmare ship, the *Neptune*, but as with all endings, it was also a beginning.

The beginning of my adventures in a new land.

The end ... and the beginning!

**Keep an eye out for Book 2 in the
Molly O'Hanlon Adventures:**

THE MYSTERY OF
THE
PARRAMATTA
FERRY

A NOTE TO OUR WONDERFUL READERS

We hope you enjoyed Molly's adventure as much as we enjoyed writing it! Molly is a fictitious character, but many of the other people and events described in the book played an important part in the history of Australia.

The Neptune was a real ship, part of the Second Fleet which transported convicts to New South Wales in the late 1700's and the evil Captain Trail was most certainly the person in charge of the ship.

John Macarthur and Captain Gilbert had a duel in front of the Fountain Hotel at Plymouth the day before the Neptune set sail, resulting in Gilbert being removed as captain and replaced by Trail.

The voyage described by Molly was also based on actual events. Many convicts died during the trip due to poor treatment, and the ship stopped at Cape Town on the way New South Wales.

And let's not forget D'Arcy Wentworth! D'Arcy left England in 1790 to sail to New South Wales on the Neptune. Although from a poor family, he managed to obtain medical training and became a doctor.

Before leaving England, D'Arcy married the still-famous author Jane Austin in a secret wedding in Scotland. They had hoped to live happily ever after.

Jane's family, however, were extremely unhappy that she had married a "rogue" such as D'Arcy – especially given the fact that he was a gambler and had even been arrested three times for highway robbery!

Although never convicted by the courts, D'Arcy thought it best to leave England and start a new life in the colonies. While in Australia, D'Arcy became a prominent and important person, recognised as someone who fought for the rights of the poor, the needy, and ... of course ... the Irish settlers.

Although he never returned to England, he and Jane wrote to each other until Jane died in 1817 – neither of them ever married anyone else ... but that's another story...

Adam & Jeff

SOME QUICK QUESTIONS

Take a look at the questions below and see if you can answer them based on the information from the book. The answers are on *Page 202*.

QUESTION 1: What was one of the main reasons England started sending convicts to New South Wales instead of to the Americas?

QUESTION 2: What is the name of the settlement at the southern tip of Africa that ships like the Neptune stopped at on their way to New South Wales and why was it important?

QUESTION 3: How long did the average voyage take from England to New South Wales in 1790?

QUESTION 4: What was the part of the Neptune called where the male convicts were kept?

QUESTION 5: Why were most of the people on the Neptune called "convicts"?

QUESTION 6: Were convicts the only ones to go to New South Wales in the late 1700's?

SOME QUICK ANSWERS

ANSWER TO QUESTION 1: Because of the American Revolution which meant that England could no longer send convicts to America.

ANSWER TO QUESTION 2: The name of the settlement is Cape Town and it was important because it marked the halfway point on the voyage from England to New South Wales, making it a perfect spot to re-supply the ships before the last leg of the trip.

ANSWER TO QUESTION 3: The trip took about 6 months with very few stops along the way!

ANSWER TO QUESTION 4: The orlop deck. The orlop deck was the lowest deck of a ship and, because it was below seal-level, it had no portholes or other access to fresh air. It was the deepest, darkest and most dreary part of the ship.

ANSWER TO QUESTION 5: They were referred to as convicts because they had been "convicted" of a crime by the courts in England. During the late 1700's and early 1800's the laws of England (and Ireland) were very harsh. People were often sentenced to death for relatively crimes such as stealing bread or even, like Tattie, pickpocketing. In many cases, the Court would replace the death sentence with a sentence of 7-years transportation, sending the convict to one of the colonies to serve their time.

ANSWER TO QUESTION 6: No. Although convicts made-up the majority of those sailing to New South Wales, others also made the voyage including the family of convicts (like Molly) government officials, soldiers (such as John Macarthur who had the duel with Captain Gilbert), and "freemen" like D'Arcy who wanted to make a new start in life.

A.J. Walfer is not a real person! Well, it kind of is, being a combination of Adam Wallace and Jeff Pfeifer!

Adam Wallace is a multiple Number 1 New York Times bestselling author, with 4 million book sales to his name. After 6 years and over 150 rejections before his first book was published, Adam now writes full-time which means he can take naps whenever he wants. When he did that as an engineer, he got in trouble. See more of Adam's books at his website: www.adam-wallace-books.com

Jeff Pfeifer is a Professor of Forensic Psychology who has worked with police, prison and justice agencies in over 35 countries. Although he has published a number of scholarly articles, chapters and books, his passion revolves around delving into the history of crime in Australia and turning this information into books for people of all ages. When Jeff takes naps at work, people just think he's a professor.

Maggie McMahon lived a swashbuckling life aboard a boat much smaller than the Neptune until she was 12, when her parents abandoned seafaring for the mainland. Now she's a landlubber living in Queensland with her husband and 2 boys. Maggie's a big fan of adventure, salty sea spray and drawing. Maggie draws a lot. If you'd like to see more of Maggie's drawings, you can visit her website: maggiemcmahonillustration.com

www.ingramcontent.com/pod-product-compliance
Lightning Source LLC
Chambersburg PA
CBHW071908220626
47052CB00002B/256

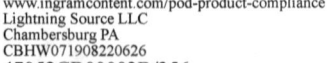